Brooklyn

Darby's Girls, Volume 3

Ella Sweetland

Published by Ella Sweetland, 2024.

This is a work of fiction. Similarities to real people, places, or events are entirely coincidental.

BROOKLYN

First edition. December 7, 2024.

Copyright © 2024 Ella Sweetland.

ISBN: 979-8227426512

Written by Ella Sweetland.

For the music and the muses who get me through

1.
Brooklyn
♪♫

BROOKLYN HUNT LAUNCHED into the last song of the night, the heat from the stage lights beading sweat on her brow. A new fear replaced the butterflies she'd had at the beginning, and she squinted at the petering crowd. What if they booed her? Or the bar earned more bad reviews for her singing like they had a few months ago.

Two Stars—Entertainment is soulless. Try some pop.
Two Stars—Worst dining experience. Manager refused to close the stage.
One Star—The 'talent' couldn't back up a back-up singer.

Just the thought shook her voice in the last bar, and she wrapped up the set with a tight smile. She had to get over it. The stage of Darby's Bar and Grill was hers, and had been for five years now. It offered security and the boost to lift her voice to follow her passion. Usually.

But the reviews were only one piece of the problem. While Darby's had proven the best home she'd ever had, the place was sinking, threatening to drown her friends in debt. Every month, the girls threw around ideas to keep the doors open—good ideas—and they worked well enough until the co-owner upped the ante.

Yvette Myers-Northam-Parker shared the bar with her daughters, Chanel and Tiffany. The Myers sisters were down-to-earth and friendly—everything their mother wasn't. They were also two of Brook's closest friends. Her cousin, Presley, had introduced her to Chanel and Pop Darby, and the rest was history. Pop and the sisters accepted everyone as family, so Brook would do anything to help the girls survive after they'd lost the patriarch a few years ago.

As she packed away her guitar and switched off the equipment, she kept her earplugs in to block out any negativity that might come her way. No one had ever heckled her live, but the anonymous words online had shaken her deep. Really, it was just one troll who'd garnered the attention of a few more—ones who'd sounded a lot like her old classmates, an ex... oh, and the manager she'd kneed in the balls.

Thankfully, the pub had emptied by the time she stepped out from the curtains, except for a table full of worried faces. The bouncer, Ronan, cradled his pregnant fiancée, who slept tucked under his chin. Their guard dog was more bark than bite, even when he glowered. "What the hell was that, Brooklyn?"

"I know it was bad." The disappointment on her friends' faces was harder to accept. *Stupid reviews.*

Chanel, the chef, handed Brooklyn tonight's dessert special—a plated brownie topped with whipped cream and caramel sauce—and waved her into a seat. "It was perfect until the last hiccup, but that's not the problem. You weren't here."

"Where was I?" Brooklyn dipped into the cream first, sampling the simple pleasure before spreading it evenly across the top.

"Somewhere in your head. The crowd loves it when you talk to them..." Chanel pushed a little pot of extra caramel sauce across the table.

"Is the review still bothering you?" Tiffany nudged her boyfriend. "Can you get rid of your sister's handiwork?"

The younger girls befriended Lucas during high school, and he'd joined Tiffany and the bar with no problems. Plus, he was smart. "Yeah, but reviews are tricky, and if customers think you're manipulating things, then it'll only get worse. You're doing well responding to the socials, but it still takes a while for things to build. Maybe we can ask our regulars to comment more, like Summer's brothers."

Eyes closed, Summer mumbled against Ronan's chest. "Stu is better suited to PR, and he visits more than Matty."

"Thought you were asleep," said Lucas.

"Just a power down until I get my husband naked." Summer burrowed closer.

Lucas groaned, but Ronan kissed her forehead, chuckling. "Not your husband yet."

"Soon enough."

Brook hoped wedding chatter would steal the spotlight, but she was out of luck, thanks to Chanel. "I won't suggest karaoke nights when there's a place down the road offering the same, but what about an open mic night? Not to replace you—that'll never happen, but involving the regulars and relieving some of the pressure might be what you need."

"Maybe." Really, what pressure did she have? No boyfriend, no family other than Presley and Aunt Vivienne. Brooklyn's mother never answered the phone, and Dad disappeared as soon as they divorced. And she only sang on Friday and Saturday nights, helping serve customers the other nights.

"I doubt anyone better than you will take the stage. You should be on the road. Are you worried about working with dodgy singers?" Chanel asked. "A lot of them will be. Drunk, too."

"No. Music is creative. Free expression and all that. What night would we try it out?" Brooklyn accepted the distraction. Changing direction had to be better than remaining static.

Tiffany checked the aqua notebook she carried everywhere. "Friday? The happy hour crowd sticks around and they'll have enough liquid courage to give it a whirl. Plus, we get the most regulars then, so they'll feel confident enough to sing with you."

"What if no one puts their hand up?" Brooklyn's confidence hit an all-time low. She thought the regulars were fans, but the self-doubt kept chipping away at her.

"Stu will give it a go. Everything he sings sounds like Bob Dylan, though," Summer said.

"What about the Tradie Ladies?" Thea asked. The women had been the sole female in their trade classes, so the electrician, plumber, mechanic, and builder had formed a little network like Darby's girls.

Power nap done, Summer straightened. "Matty and Stu have worked with Lainey and Pippa. They never shut up about Pip."

Suddenly exhausted from the worry, Brook sighed. "Next Friday then. Sorry..."

"No!" the group chorused, cutting off her apology.

Lucas shook his head. "If anyone should apologise, it's me. Leah has hurt all you girls, except for Pres."

"Yeah, she did. When Presley fronted her about the non-payment, Leah reported her to the head of her firm," said Brooklyn, although Pres refused to back down to anyone, so the complaint hadn't progressed past a chat with her boss. The same boss who loved Presley's no-nonsense approach.

"At least Leah's under house arrest now." Lucas shredded a napkin. "Mum and Dad might finally realise how bad she was to live with—the lies."

"She should be in jail." Tears warbled Tiffany's voice, and she rubbed a hand over Lucas' shoulder that had taken a knife.

Chanel squeezed her sister. "I think we're all exhausted, so let's break up the party."

The others drifted off, leaving Brook and Chanel alone. Chanel hugged her. "You always have a place here, Brook. And you could easily tour, fantastically, but you'd be welcome home whenever you wanted."

"I like my life here, and touring seems exhausting." Imagine the reviews if she took on the world...

Chanel squeezed tighter. "I get it. I just don't want you to add to the worries. We'll never ask you to leave."

A WEEK LATER, BROOK loitered behind the black curtains as she set up her stage, ready for the open mic gig. Lucas had adjusted their social page, with a list of rules so he could remove comments without prejudice, and had given her an extra task to log on each day to promote the gig and interact with their followers. Sometimes she worried it was fake, or at least forced, but as the week wore on, she'd had fun with it.

Now she needed to walk that enthusiasm out onto the stage.

2.
Hudson

HUDSON WELLS WAITED in front of the bar that his mate, Eli, wanted to check out. Eli hadn't given a reason for the visit, but Hudson knew him well—it was either money or a woman. Eli was easy to spot amongst the Friday evening crowd, not just for his six-foot something height. He still wore a business suit, while Hudson was underdressed in jeans and a surf shirt.

Eli sat his glasses on top of his head before they shook hands. "Just get out of bed?"

"Yeah, fuck you. First to throw out an insult buys dinner, remember?"

"And the first to swear buys the beers," Eli added. The rules had come about over a decade ago, when their circle of friends included a few others. They were long gone.

Hudson lifted his sunglasses onto his messy hair and scanned the pub built early last century. Bottle green tiles covered the bottom quarter of the red brick walls that seemed infused with the smell of beer and nicotine. "When did you take an interest in ancient relics?"

"I've heard whispers about the place, and I was curious. A pair of sisters co-own it."

"This should be fun," Hudson muttered under his breath and earned a glare. Eli was good with money and women—separately. Mix the two together and the guy found himself in a mess every time.

They entered to find happy hour in full swing and joined the wait at the bar. At one end, the bouncer leant across the oak-top bar, arguing with a petite blonde, who was lucky to reach his chin. She smiled serenely at his blustering before a redhead pulling beers interrupted the couple.

"Two more hours behind the bar, Summer. Ronan, you'll have dinner together, then let her rest until you're done," she said. When the pierced and tattooed guy pouted, she pointed at him. "The bar is between the crowd and your babies, so go pretend you work here."

Ronan made a point of kissing the object of his frustration and left her blushing. The redhead greeted Hudson and Eli. "Welcome to Darby's, I'm Tiffany. What can I get you?"

Eli straightened—first target acquired, apparently. Hudson ignored him and answered. "A couple of light beers to start. Any other entertainment scheduled tonight?"

"Ha! They are entertaining." The girl grinned, and a dimple flashed. "We have our regular musician playing a set later if you're sticking around."

"We will." Eli snapped out of his assessment and switched on the charm. "Who's the chef tonight?"

"My sister, Chanel. How did you hear about us?" Tiffany asked as she expertly filled two pint glasses.

"Your ads have popped up everywhere. The winery ones..." Eli trailed off and pointed above the bar. "Same artist?"

Tiffany set the drinks on the bar, then nudged the blushing blonde. "Summer did both. She hasn't quite realised she's an artist yet. And my boyfriend's an IT pro, so he's worked some magic to ensure the ads pop up frequently."

"You have a good team. We'll let you work," said Eli, lifting the drinks as Hudson waved his bank card.

Tiffany smiled politely. "Thanks. The girls are always on the floor, so if you need anything, just ask."

Guessing Eli wanted to check out the other sister, Hudson figured he might as well scope out the music, so they found a table towards the back and close to the stage and the kitchen. He hadn't performed or written music in ages and only played his guitar an hour or so a day to keep the callouses on his fingertips.

After a few beers they ordered some food, and lowlights turned on behind the stage curtain. A small gap showed a figure moving in the shadows, but nothing defining. When the bouncer and his girlfriend walked past the stage, another blonde woman stepped out from behind the curtains and down the few steps to greet them, teasing a frown from the broody man and a giggle from Summer. Whoever she was, the woman was another member of the tight-knit group.

He and Eli used to enjoy the support of a wide circle of friends, but had experienced the damage and divisiveness when things didn't go to plan.

The delivery of the Friday night special—fish and chips—stole their focus, and Hudson caught Eli frowning over the perfect pub meal. Hudson kicked him. "What's your problem? Are you looking for faults in this setup?"

"There's another bar Dad's added to our portfolio, and I wanted to check out the competition. This place received similar reviews a few months ago, but... it doesn't make sense." Eli poked at the meal, then worked out his insulin dosage before discretely jabbing himself.

After one memorable trip to the emergency room, Hudson always waited for Eli to finish before distracting him. "Why doesn't it make sense?"

"The bad reviews for the other place are legit, but the comments for this place don't fit." Eli zipped his medication wallet and tucked it in the pocket of his suit jacket. "Food, service, and style are all up there."

"What else does your ream of research tell you?" Hudson asked. Eli would've done a complete history of the place before looking—it was his way.

"The sisters inherited the place from their grandfather. Tiffany and Summer have been best friends since school, along with another waitress. Chanel's best friend is their accountant, whose cousin floats around filling in wherever. Chanel's side of the friendly tree has higher privacy settings."

"I don't blame them. There's a fine line between research and stalking, bro."

Eli threw back an insult, but the stage had finally opened, and Hudson settled in for a familiar rush. Hopefully good music, but amateurs didn't bother him—live music was life. The blonde that wasn't Summer stepped up to the microphone, and Hudson shifted in his seat.

Eli groaned. "No. Down, boy."

Hudson swore at him and ordered another round as the woman welcomed the crowd. "We're mixing things up tonight, guys. I think you're all getting bored with me..."

She didn't finish because a few groups protested loudly, but she settled them with a raised hand and continued. "Tonight,

I'll run through a few of my favourites, then if any of you think you're up for it, you can let me take you for a test drive—you go solo, then do it with me."

The suggestion straightened Hudson, and once again Eli uttered a desperate denial. Hudson shut Eli out and lost himself in the girl on stage. A few songs were backed digitally, but she played most of the set on an acoustic guitar with as much skill as he played electric. Then there was her voice—she had a range from high octane to sultry smooth. Maybe he did need Eli to stop him from storming the stage tonight.

Hudson channelled Eli, and picked apart her style throughout the set, but when she welcomed others onto the stage, he knew no one else could match her as well as he could. Eli smacked him upside the head.

"What the hell?" Hudson growled.

Eli rolled his eyes. "We have an agreement... you're not to collaborate with women ever again."

"She's fucking awesome," said Hudson, and took another hit. He watched a few more men and women embarrass themselves before they called it a night. Hudson wasn't ready for that and raised his hand. "Got time for one more?"

A group of drunk idiots helped him out by calling for an encore, and she held back a grin. "The fans have spoken, so come on up."

"You're on your own, bro." Eli shook his head and stood. "I'm heading out, but if you need bail money or someone to sit with you through recovery, call me."

Hudson smiled at the joke that was too close to the truth, then revelled in taking the stage for the first time in forever. The girl's friendly stage presence vanished when she greeted him. "I hope you have some songs in mind…"

"Can I borrow your guitar?" Hudson asked.

She narrowed her eyes. "Sure, but first rule: if you break it, you've bought it."

"I won't. Here are a few songs I know you can handle. I've chosen one I want to do you, but you can pick one to challenge me." He handed over the little pad he always carried in case his muse ever returned.

"Who says I need a challenge?" The girl was tough.

"You did, thinking you're boring the crowd. What's your name?"

"Brook mostly, Brooklyn when I'm in trouble."

Hudson raised his eyebrows and stepped away to text Eli. Someone had set him up. Without a response, he had to follow through and played the first cover. Not his best work. Brooklyn's face softened, and when he'd finished two more songs, he pulled her aside. "Do you know a guy called Eli?"

"Should I?"

"You're Brooklyn, I'm Hudson. Sounds premeditated."

She shrugged. "Think what you want, but you promised a challenge, so get on with it."

Hudson shut down his twitching and launched into a riff everyone would know. Brooklyn rolled her eyes, but her body found the rhythm and when the song asked her for the time, she snapped back without losing a beat. *"I miss you more than anything."*

The song about lovers on opposite sides of the world was fun and light, but she made it sound like the female lead couldn't care less about the separation. As they wound down, Hudson bit back a smile—the princess didn't do pop. They bent their heads together over the list and he held his breath.

"This one isn't a duet," said Brooklyn, pointing at the one he wanted her to choose.

Hudson brought up the lyrics on his phone. "We do the chorus together. I'll take the first verse, you the second and first two lines of the third. You're not a fucking backup singer."

When she paled, he almost apologised, but with one sharp nod, she gave him what he wanted.

3.
Brooklyn

BROOK CHECKED OVER the lyrics of the sultry soul song as Hudson scrawled notations on a scrap of paper. The guy knew music, probably lived it more than she did, and he was better than good—an unexpected gem in the rough crowd. Although he blended in. Blond like herself, his hair long enough to tie back while the curls at the back brushed the torn neck of his surf shirt. Muscle corded his arms, and his height had him readjusting her guitar strap for a better fit.

He met her gaze, and she tried to ignore the ocean blue depths by focussing on his stubble. Gees, the mouth.

"What do you think?" Hudson asked.

"Nice."

A smile quirked the full lips. "You'll do it?"

Shit, the song... "Yeah, let's go."

She turned, but he stopped her with a hand across her waist—over-friendly, but all too tempting. "You'll go with me, Brooklyn. Match my sound and let loose."

"I'll be higher."

"Just how it should be. No shallows, use your depth."

When she focussed on the crowd, she spotted Ronan first. Hard not to when he was built like a back-rower, and he wasn't smiling, just curiosity furrowing his brow. Summer and Thea leant against the end of the bar closest to the stage, and even

Chanel stood in the kitchen's doorway. Hudson had captured everyone's attention.

She cleared her throat, but Hudson bent that mouth to the mic. "Test drive's over, baby. Let's take it home."

The Dark End of the Street's intro of three simple notes hushed the crowd, and he launched into the first verse, his voice huskier than the pop songs he'd glossed over. He definitely had soul. Depth. She joined him at the chorus, entwining her voice with his and adding a little rasp to suit the song. To suit him.

This couldn't end well.

When she stole the spotlight for the next verse, she closed her eyes and went with it. The attention never bothered her, but the focus from the man next to her pulsed between them. Then she met his gaze for the chorus, just in time to catch his little smirk, and she almost stumbled through the added riff before it was her turn again. They ended with another chorus together, neither of them smiling now as they searched each other's faces.

There was a heartbeat of silence when the music ended, and their forgotten audience erupted. People called for more, but Hudson raised his hand. "Sorry, guys, she's worn me out. I'll leave you with the star of the show."

The undeserved praise had her following him to the edge of the stage. "Thanks..."

"No problem." Before the total brush-off, he turned a troubled frown on her. "Are you sure you don't know Eli?"

"Never met anyone by that name."

Hudson stepped down but gazed up at her. "Who have you worked with in the industry? You're not just a pub singer."

"A guy who should be in jail. I think he moved on to selling boats." Thinking about her manager—now stepfather—raised her hackles too easily.

His mouth flatlined. "I might come back."

"Why? You're not a pub gig, either."

Shaking his head, Hudson grabbed his jacket from the table and strode away through the crowd, good-naturedly accepting the pats on the back. And he didn't look back.

Good one, Brook.

As the bar emptied, she sang another few songs, but it wasn't the same. She felt hollowed out and adrift without him, and that alone was the perfect reason to send him away. But she hadn't sung with someone for years—hadn't wanted to, if she were honest. Brook packed up behind the shield of curtains, then sat on an amp once she was done trying to settle herself.

Time to tell her friends she'd instructed the answer to their problems to not come back. And of course they were waiting for her, eyes goggling over radiant smiles.

Chanel squeezed her tight. "Where has he been all your life? There's some magic there."

"I don't think he'll be back."

"Sure he will." Thea reached out with a slip of paper. "He left you his number. Before you freak, no, I didn't give him yours."

"Thanks. I don't think we'll top that next week." She pocketed the scrap of paper, ignoring the weight of those ten numbers.

"The patrons loved it before the superstar performance, and we can prove it because the socials went wild with the tags and comments." Tiffany grinned, almost bouncing on the spot.

Lucas waved his phone. "They're heating up now, even videos."

"Oh, god." Brook groaned.

"It was great, honey, the banter and the singing. It was as if you've worked together before." Chanel hugged her tight. "He'll turn up."

HE SHOWED ON WEDNESDAY. A quiet night, mainly serving Pop's cronies who'd remained loyal since he'd passed. Hudson ordered a beer from Thea, then turned to Brook. "Do you get a break?"

Thea jumped in. "Take her to a booth and I'll bring your drinks over."

"Oh, god… ignore her." Brook pleaded.

Hudson chuckled. "I have three younger sisters, so stickybeaks don't put me off. Have a drink with me, please."

She took him to a corner booth away from the others, and he let her sit first before joining her. "Did Thea pass on my number? After she threatened to use it herself…"

"Yeah, I made sure she didn't put it in her phone first. We're not sisters, but the six of us are close. One is my cousin."

"Chanel and Tiffany are sisters…" Hudson nodded. "My mate, Eli, wanted to check out the bar, and he mentioned them. He was comparing it to some bar he was looking to buy."

"Darby's isn't for sale." Brook straightened, ready to defend her friends if Yvette had gone behind their backs.

"That's cool. No one knows what Eli is thinking until he's done it—not even him sometimes." Hudson sipped his beer and relaxed in the seat. "He doesn't know you, either. Sorry, I was paranoid."

"No problem. Did you see the socials? A lot of people thought it was a setup, so you're not alone in your paranoia."

"What about you?" Hudson asked.

"My friends wouldn't mess with me like that. They know I've struggled lately, and the open mic was to take the pressure off." She excused herself when she caught Summer about to lift a case of wine and took over the job for a few moments.

When she returned to Hudson, his beer had almost gone. "Sorry, we have to watch her. She forgets she's having twins sometimes."

"You're all tight." Hudson sighed. "And we're fucking brilliant together."

"If you want to come back…"

"Probably shouldn't, but I don't make the best choices. See you soon." He drained his beer and left her with a peck on the cheek and the horrible emptiness.

And he didn't show Friday, or the one after. Hudson was gone.

4.
Brooklyn

THE FOLLOWING MONDAY, Brook missed half of the monthly meeting where Yvette swanned in, demanded Chanel and Tiffany to buy her out for the thousandth time—because that's how mothers behave, apparently—then left them deflated. Oh, and at least two of the group earned some derogatory comment along the way. First Summer copped a mouthful for her unwedded mother-to-be state, then she almost outed Presley's past.

Chanel covered Pres, while Ronan ushered Yvette away from his fiancée and out the front door. In the past, he'd found great pleasure in bouncing the woman, but now she just irritated them all. Like a persistent rash.

When Ronan returned to soothe Summer, she sighed. "I know we could tell her the wedding is next month, but I really don't want her to come."

"Neither do we, summertime." Tiffany squeezed her hand. The three younger women were almost sisters, while Brook had always been the odd one out. It didn't bother her. Not often, anyway.

Summer peered around Ronan. "Can you sing at the wedding, Brook? Bring Hudson—you two are awesome together."

"You want Hudson there, but not Yvette?" Brook teased, knowing anyone would take precedence over Yvette. Hudson might be an unknown, but Brook wouldn't mind his company, either.

"I like him, and the way you sing together is awesome." Summer snickered, a big change from the ghost of a girl she'd become before Ronan. "Mum does not like Yvette—brings out the sweariness in her."

"Mrs Thomas doesn't swear." Brook scoffed.

Ronan grinned. "It takes a bit, but when she loosens up, the family roasts are fun. So you need to come up with the next fundraiser, Brooklyn."

"Why?" She almost whined, unwilling to organise a Christmas event when she'd avoided the holiday for years. "Christmas is always busy, we'll be fine. And there are only so many open mic nights we can do. Hasn't that given us a boost?"

"Yeah, and with each success, Mum's self-worth inflates, and she puts up the price. Why was she hassling you, Pres?" Tiffany broke a cookie and offered half to Lucas.

Presley met Brook's gaze. Years ago, they'd worked together in a seedy club, and neither had the desire to relive the days. But...

"Those kinds of classes are growing, Pres."

"I know, but..." Presley dumped at least four teaspoons of sugar into her coffee, pouting as she stirred. "Nick won't like it."

Lucas grimaced. "Should Ronan and I leave?"

"We kept our clothes on." Brook's matter-of-fact answer flushed Lucas' cheeks, and even Ronan fidgeted.

Paying extra attention to removing all the cookie crumbs, Lucas nodded. "Ah, cool. Not strippers."

"Lucas, honey..." Tiffany covered his hand and shook her head, so Lucas could apologise before Presley threw something at him.

Ronan grumbled beside Summer. "Pop used to worry about you, and I don't think it's a good idea. Imagine the insurance, and the risks—alcohol and pole dancing?"

"You've worked in gyms that have classes." Brook aimed a kick at him. "And is the liability insurance any different to you offering personal training at the local park?"

"I still need permission. If you can, then I'll support it, obviously. Thankfully Summer can't join." Ronan relaxed a little, but Summer cut off the grinning idiot with a jab to the ribs.

Presley glowered, too. "And how did you know Ronan?"

"Pop told me. Said if I ever stepped foot in that club, he'd skin me alive." Despite rubbing his ribs, Ronan kissed away Summer's cranky scowl.

Chanel raised a hand. "We'll put it in the maybe column and look at it in the new year, but I agree with Brook. There's plenty of action during the holidays, and if Hudson sticks around, then we can pull bigger crowds on the weekend. Only if you're okay with that, though. Personally, I think you're great solo, and don't want to change the dynamic."

"Test it out for a few weeks, and I'll compare the nights. Although Friday is often busier." Tiffany flicked through her notebook to an empty page before scribbling in it.

The bar depended on them all working together, so Brook plucked up some courage. "I'll run it by Hudson. I don't know if he was after a regular gig."

"Do you still have his number?" Chanel scrunched her nose with the sneaky question.

"I do." Ignoring the curiosity, she texted him then helped Summer clean away the coffee remnants.

He rang her almost an hour later.

"Did I disturb you?" Brooklyn asked.

"Nah, I had a burst of creativity, so I've been messing around in my studio." Of course, he had a studio. Just his talent piqued her interest, but she hadn't looked him up, no matter how much she wanted to.

"Can we meet somewhere? I need to ask you something."

His voice dropped low. "You can't say it over the phone?"

"I like to see people's faces when I ask for something, otherwise they just agree, then hate you for asking later."

"Huh! We must have met the same people in the past. Want to see my studio?" The gruff voice sounded like he was offering something else. Something much more interesting than guitar amps and sound booths.

Curiosity won, and she cleared her throat. "Text me your address and I'll be there soon. If you have time—I need to get back for opening."

"Sure. See you soon."

The text popped up a few minutes later, and she grabbed her gear from the locker. Chanel caught her on the way out. "Do you feel safe with him?"

"He's low risk. I should be back to open, but... I'll give you his address." Brook forwarded the text, then mumbled. "Thanks, Chanel."

"Hey, you're ours. I'm worried about Pres, too. She's hiding more than you."

Aunt Viv had been a hard woman to live with—harder than Brook's mother—and despite finding a husband who adored her,

Presley had faded. "Respect is important, especially after a childhood of disrespect and neglect. She was a freaking awesome dancer, though. If we can swing it, the classes would be good for her, and she'd be a better teacher."

"Give me an idea of what we might need, then we'll hit her with a proper plan," said Chanel, on the move again and ready to prep for the night. "Go have fun. I'll send out a search party if I don't hear from you."

Brooklyn left shaking her head at herself, not Chanel. How stupid to think she was on her own?

Fifteen minutes later, she stood at Hudson's front door, knocking for the seventh time. She ended up sending another text, and he appeared around the side of the house.

"Hey, the studio's at the back." Dressed only in boxer shorts with his hair falling from the tie, he could've just left his bed.

She really had to stop thinking about Hudson and bed at the same time. "Looks like I woke you up."

As she trailed him around the verandah, he checked himself out. "Shit. Sorry, I'll grab some clothes."

The old federation home had a shady porch, wide enough for a surfboard rack. A collection of thongs waited beside the mat, but otherwise, the space was neat. Down the yard, a new granny flat peeked out from behind a weatherboard shed.

Hudson reappeared in jeans, pulling a t-shirt over his head and covering the sculpted body. Afterwards, he shook out his hair, then tightened the band back around the waves as he explained. "When the stick hits, I get lost for a while, but it hasn't happened for a long time. I don't think I've eaten, either."

"Do you have eggs and bread?" When he nodded, Brook sighed. "Show me your studio, then I'll cook you breakfast."

5.
Hudson

HUDSON TOOK HER INTO his pride and joy, although the studio had offered little joy until today. Working with the woman had knocked a few cobwebs free, and he'd written a sheet of music around three am. He was up to five pages now. Brooklyn's eyes widened as she circled the room. One of the mixing boards earned a reverent stroke, while his favourite guitar was ogled with a serious case of yearning.

"Want to test it out?" Hudson asked, enjoying the smile lighting her eyes.

She shook her head, though. "God, no, I might break it."

"You break it, you've bought it."

"That's right. And it'd take me ten years to pay you back. You've written some comps." Brooklyn craned her neck, but didn't intrude.

The night they'd met, he'd found it difficult to keep a distance between them, but old wounds had him gathering the manuscript to hide in a file. "What did you want to ask me?"

"Oh, the bar is trying to boost funds to buy out Tiff and Chanel's mother. We're arguing whether taking on another musician will give it a boost." She dragged her gaze from the photos of him on stage.

"What side are you on?"

"I don't know." Flushing, her gaze dropped to the floor. "A couple of months ago there was a review on my poor singing, which is why we tried the open mic the other week."

"The review had to be bullshit. You don't need me to back you up." Although he stepped closer, he tucked his hands in his pockets before doing something he'd regret. Like hold on to her for dear life.

"I enjoy singing with you, though." Her cheeks glowed brighter as she muttered. "Chanel doesn't want to change the dynamics, but I think you'd add an extra layer. That's if you're interested."

Since she was still looking everywhere but at him, he pushed back. "I thought you wanted to see my reaction."

Then she turned a stunning smile his way. "Your playroom is a distraction. Maybe I don't want you to see my disappointment when you say no."

Figuring full disclosure hadn't played a part in most of his past collaborations with women, he opted for honesty. "I might have ulterior motives if I agree."

"Such as?" Her mouth tightened a little. Someone had burnt her, too.

He opened up a little, hoping the trust wouldn't fail him later. "I haven't sung live in too long, and after you, I can hear music again. New stuff, and I think it's good. How many nights are we talking?"

"Friday and Saturday maybe into the new year. We haven't thought about that yet. Although, we're floating a plan to offer pole dancing classes."

"No shit? How do you get a teacher for that?"

"A friend and I used to back in the day. Clothes on."

"I'm sure you didn't need to strip to cause a stir." A vivid blush stained her cheeks, confusing him. Where had the cool woman disappeared to? He held her hand before she ran. "So if you be my muse for a while, I can play with you Friday and Saturdays—no charge."

"Seriously?"

Hudson nodded, reminding himself not to tell Eli that bit, if any. He'd be on his case for sure, because in Eli's world, nothing was given freely. The woman stared longingly at his Gibson again, so he nudged her. "I'm in, Brooklyn. Come make me breakfast before your drooling rusts the strings."

Laughter rang out, as stunning as the smile. "Okay. Thank you."

"No problem. We need to work on a song list." He dug out an empty pad from his crowded desk and searched for a pencil.

"Behind your ear..." Brook pointed at him. "I thought you knew what songs I could sing."

"True, but I don't enjoy playing the same stuff over and over, so we need a few sets. I could teach music if I was desperate enough, but hearing twenty kids a week slaughter 'Smoke on the Water' would do my head in." Maybe he'd have to teach soon, especially if Dad kept pushing Hudson to leave the recording business and return to live performances.

"Hey, it's a classic. Oh, Summer asked if you could play at their wedding, too. Just for the party, not the bridal march. Mr Thomas is paying—he's old school."

God, she was leading him in deeper, and he couldn't refuse. "So I'd just turn up for the party."

"You can come with me, unless you have an aversion to weddings."

"I don't think so—I've never been to one."

Back in the house, she moved gracefully around his kitchen, and the news she could dance wasn't surprising. The pole dancing revelation had blindsided him, but that was athleticism as much as grace and sensuality. A swift crack to the egg, and she dumped it in the bowl one-handed, chatting again as she moved onto the next. "Summer almost married in September, but the guy jilted her."

"Did she cheat on him?"

She scorched him with a glare. "Ahh, no. The jerk cheated on her, actually. The twins make her look more pregnant than she is."

"I know less about that stuff than weddings."

"Ronan and Summer's wedding will be low key like them. No drama, and they'll call time early because those babies wear her out already."

When she only cooked two slices of toast, he frowned. "Aren't you eating?"

"I ate breakfast at seven-thirty."

"Can't it be lunch?" Hudson asked hopefully. He wasn't ready for her to leave. "And how do you expect me to eat four eggs?"

"You're a guy. Ronan drinks four raw ones. It's hideous."

"I'm hungry, don't ruin my appetite."

Brook added an extra slice of bread into the toaster, then stirred the scrambling eggs.

"I like the way you move, Brooklyn. As much as your voice. Why are you playing pub gigs?" He kept his eyes on her, looking for any little tell that would give him more clues.

The woman could clam up tighter than anyone he'd known, considering every word before she spoke. "One pub. Pop Darby was a lifesaver when no one else turned up for me."

"I reckon he would've wanted you to fly higher."

"He did, and for a while I was out there." Smacking the wooden spoon on the edge of the pan, she left it to scrape butter on the golden toast. "When I hit that high, my manager wanted to cash in differently, and when I didn't give him what he wanted, I was relegated to backup singer."

Hudson shook his head. After her reaction when he told her otherwise, he should've expected that insult. "You didn't give in, did you?"

Her busyness ramped up with the uncomfortable topic, and she dumped eggs over his toast, then slid the plate across the bench. "No, I can be stubborn, and he probably couldn't hassle anyone else for a couple of weeks. Hopefully, his wife noticed his blue balls and got out."

He nearly choked on a mouthful of eggs with his laughter. "Savage. Good work."

She closed herself off a little more, and he could've kicked himself. "I'm sorry. It's not funny when it happens too often. The entitlement and the threats."

"That's in the past, but I don't promote myself as Darby's entertainment—I'm just there for my friends. Attention isn't my goal."

Hudson held out a hand to shake on it. "Same goes."

HUDSON SECOND-GUESSED himself a handful of times before their first full gig together. Whenever he suffered uncertainty, he would talk to Eli or his closest sister, Shannon. He'd kept it quiet, though, not because he was ashamed. During the week, he'd shared lunch with Brooklyn and there was something between them besides their love for music—something he wanted to nurture despite the many women who'd betrayed him. Honestly, he didn't know how he always chose the wrong women. None of his sisters or their mother held back, all preferring to tackle issues head-on, and perhaps they'd made him complacent—it had taken a long time to figure out that not all women were the same.

Brooklyn was different again, and when he stepped up beside her behind the stage curtains, the once wary smile now shone. "Hey, I'm glad you came..."

"Did you think I wouldn't?" Hudson unzipped his guitar bag and pulled out his electric, then the lead and their notes from the front pocket.

After hooking up his lead to an amp, she tipped her head at him. "Sometimes I think you're holding back. Not that I can judge."

"Like recognises like... I'm okay, Brook. I want to be here."

He regretted the confident reassurance an hour later. Everything was on fire—the crowd, the woman who didn't mind leading or backing him, sharing the spotlight effortlessly. And he burned for her, too, an ache in his soul he had to keep in check just in case the entire world saw how much he wanted her.

Pausing for a drink from their water bottles between the final sets, she softly spoke beside him. "You're doing well. Why are you retreating?"

"The crowd's huge tonight. Have you added my name to the social posts?"

"No. We agreed this was for the bar, not us." Brook squeezed his hand. "Join me in the depths."

AFTER ANOTHER FEW WEEKS of playing together, he'd taken to wearing baggier surf shirts to hide his perpetual hard-on, but damn, he was happy. Soul-deep, and he now had a completed manuscript book. Brooklyn Hunt was more than a muse, and a hell of a lot more than the other women he'd believed were the one. And from the light that bloomed in her face more every passing day, he guessed she felt pretty positive about the shift, too.

He stepped behind the stage curtain and found her sitting on an amp, scrolling through her phone with a frown. She stood quickly, apologising.

"What's wrong?"

"Apparently, some girls wanted your number the other night, and Lucas told them we're together. Now they're dragging me in the socials... I'm back to 'talentless' and 'can't back up a backup singer'. Lucas used our community guidelines to remove the posts, but they're reviewing on other sites. I'm sorry."

"For what? You're not responsible for their behaviour."

"Lucas shouldn't have lied."

"Is it a lie? I probably would've said I'm seeing someone, too, and you're the only woman I want to see." He held her hand and drew her closer, but not so much that she'd freak out. "Were you reading the reviews just now?"

"I know I shouldn't..."

"Delete them, Brooklyn. You're so much more than someone's petty opinion." For a moment, he thought she'd refused, but she followed through with shaky hands, and he kissed her cheek. "Am I still your wedding date tomorrow? Cos in my eyes, we're not just a gig."

"Yes, please."

6.
Brooklyn

THE NEXT MORNING, BROOKLYN worked at the Thomas' vineyard, setting up for the night of entertainment once Summer tied Ronan in a few more knots. While Presley often told the couple they looked ridiculous together, and really it was an unexpected match, they were perfect for each other. Summer softened the burly man to putty, and Ronan only needed to hold her hand to have her shining as bright as her name.

Summer had grown up here, her family solid with well-established roots like the gnarled rows of vines. Since Brooklyn's dad abandoned her, she'd learnt to watch people carefully. There was a difference between Summer's relationship and her cousin's. Presley and Nick loved each other without a doubt, but there was some kind of communication glitch that didn't fill Brook with confidence. Maybe the upbringing she and Presley shared was the problem—parents who didn't give a crap.

Because the Thomas' were tight-knit, they'd supported Summer through her ordeal with the ex-asshole who'd sapped her joy, and Brook realised the wrong people could poison anyone's roots. Then there were Summer's brothers, who had a peculiar interest in sharing a woman between them. That chestnut—a hot one—didn't faze the Thomas' at all. They loved their kids unconditionally.

Despite knowing Matt and Stu's rare outlook on relationships, when the electrician, Pippa, turned up dressed for a wedding but prepared to help, Brook couldn't stem her curiosity. "Who are you dating? Matt or Stu?"

Pippa blushed, but just as quickly, she puffed up with courage. "Both. I'm theirs."

"Good. If Mrs Thomas let you help, then you're pretty much family."

Pippa just shrugged. "She mentioned the Thomas men prefer efficiency over safety."

"There's an overloaded power board under the drinks table."

"For the love of god."

Once Pippa left, Brook finished the setup and hurried to the room Mrs Thomas had given her for the night. It wasn't big or flashy, but the homey feel soothed her. While the apartment Pop had left her was comfortable, it wasn't quite right. She'd felt too damn comfortable at Hudson's place. That, followed by all the nights they'd played together, had taken her to a new level of comfort.

Brooklyn slipped into her little black dress, then joined her friends to fuss over Summer. She kept her eye on the driveway outside, waiting for Hudson's car to appear.

When he turned up for the ceremony without the surfer look, she was lost for words for too long. The black chinos—no holes—were paired with a charcoal shirt that turned his ocean eyes stormy. The intense perusal flushed his cheeks, so she soothed him. "You look good. I don't mind the jeans and t-shirt—or the boxer shorts."

"I'll save those for you. Are you a bridesmaid?" He held her hand while his gaze caressed its way down her body. "This dress is a killer."

"No, Tiff and Thea are the bridesmaids. You only get me. Not so fancy." She straightened the black satin spaghetti strap that refused to sit right.

His mouth tightened for a moment. "You're perfect. I had to borrow this shirt from my mate. Sorry, I wasn't here for the setup."

"Most was done for me." She led him down the aisle and joined Chanel and Presley.

Underneath the arch swathed in a rainbow of roses and trailing leaves, Ronan chatted with the Thomas brothers and Lucas, who seemed more nervous than the groom. Hudson muttered beside her. "Guess it's not a shotgun wedding. Ronan looks pretty chill."

Chanel tipped her head. "Someone has to take a photo of him when he sees her."

"He won't cry," Presley scoffed.

"No, but we need proof," said Chanel. The girls had formed a betting pool a few weeks ago, and Brooklyn and Chanel had picked him to cry.

Hudson frowned between the women. "Proof of what?"

"That love exists," Chanel joked.

Presley pouted. "It does when it turns up."

Then the music swelled, and the crowd turned in their seats. Brook faced the front, though, with her phone's camera pointed at the men. She captured Lucas first, his tension melting away when Tiffany joined them at the altar. After that, he couldn't take his eyes off her, not when Thea arrived or the moment

Ronan straightened beside him. She caught the lift of Ronan's eyebrows, and the pure joy in his smile, before he rubbed a hand over his heart.

Oh, yeah—there's the love. She turned back in time to snap Summer beaming just as bright, then the back of her as the bride reached the altar. As Ronan pressed his thumb and forefinger into his tear-ducts, Chanel muttered a 'told-you-so'.

Presley hissed back. "That's not crying."

"Close enough."

When Mr Thomas kissed Summer's cheek and left her with Ronan, the couple fused together, lost in their own little world until the celebrant cleared her throat. Brooklyn had only attended Presley's wedding, but hadn't listened closely to the vows. This time she absorbed it all: the shared looks of understanding, the seriousness, and emotion—proof that love did exist. After the 'I dos' and congratulations, the family wandered off for photos.

The rest stayed at the cellar door, set up for the dinner and party. Hudson grabbed a light beer, but Brooklyn stuck with soft drink and they settled together at a bar table overlooking the vineyard. The wired fences supporting the vines reminded her of a music stave, all neat and orderly.

"Nice place."

Since it was one of her favourite places, she nodded. "The Thomas' have grown a few generations here."

"Would you do the wedding thing?" Hudson asked.

"Once upon a time, no way, but Ronan was dead-set against marriage, and now I think the right person changes everything. In a good way. My friends are the only family I have, so it'd be a small wedding if it ever happened." She burned up with the confession, wondering how she gave him too much information again. "What about you?"

"I told you about the three younger sisters, and we have a huge extended family. They're great, but the bigger the family, the more opinions you face." He caught her frowning at his brush off and sighed. "My parents have a good marriage, so yeah, I'd want the right person, too."

Before she could overthink, he clasped her hand, only letting go when necessary, and they settled into the celebrations.

After dinner and the speeches, it was time for them to take the stage. The crowd was no bigger than the pubs, but nerves skittered through her. The set list was all love songs and duets, and the more they played, the more the crowd receded. By the time they were halfway through, she believed every word they sang.

Hudson changed guitars, but before the opening, he covered the microphone, blocking her from the audience as he murmured. "If you keep looking at me like that, I'll forget where we are."

"Where are we?"

His lips quirked before he dropped them to hers for a moment. "Right on the edge."

A few songs later, she missed the opening, and he covered her until she caught up. At the end, he slung his guitar behind his back. "Fuck it."

Hudson framed her face, his fingers tangling in her hair, before another brush of his lips turned into a desperate tangle—a duet to a duel. She circled his waist, hoping the hug would keep her grounded. Eventually, his hands dropped to her waist to anchor their bodies, and he took her deeper, under and away from the lights and music. Until he pulled back, and snippets of reality crept back in, along with the wolf whistles and cheering from her friends.

He groaned against her ear. "Are any of your friends gunning for me? I grabbed you."

She answered by urging his mouth back to hers and initiating another kiss. Then they continued with the set like nothing happened, except they couldn't stop looking at each other, or the smiles just for them.

Once the set was done, they set aside the microphone and guitar and left the stage hand-in-hand. While the crowd called for an encore, they hid behind a tent, and she ended up back in his arms.

Eventually, she whimpered. "They want more."

"So do I. Come back to my place." In full-on seduction mode, he nuzzled from her neck down to her cleavage.

"Summer and Ronan haven't left yet. I think there's a rule..."

Hudson raised his head, his eyes dark and glittering. "Okay, we'll have a drink, but you need to cover me."

"Why?"

When he pulled her tight against his hard-on, she tiptoed for a better fit. A growl rumbled through him. "That doesn't help. You're supposed to cover me, not climb me."

"Feels good, you make me feel good."

"We'll feel much better when we have a bed. I won't do you against a wall or in a public bathroom."

"Such a gentleman... although 'do' me?"

"Loving you. I'll make love to you and rock your damn world."

Their hopeful plans were waylaid as they hung around to help tidy up after the newlyweds and guests left. Chanel had taken an inebriated Presly home, leaving Tiffany, Lucas, and Thea to help the Thomas'. By one a.m., Brooklyn was wiped, so they stayed in the guest room. She didn't expect their first night together to be half-dressed, with no touching allowed.

Hudson tossed and turned for a while until she hissed at him. "Are you always so restless?"

"I've never had an erection for hours before. It's uncomfortable."

"Well, think bad thoughts." She was, and just thinking about seeking relief against his body had her just as restless. "We're in someone else's home."

"Hard for hours, Brooklyn." When Thea's muffled snort sounded from the room next door, he stilled before heaving a sigh. "Fine. Tomorrow."

7.
Brooklyn

SUNLIGHT FLOODED THE guest room, and Hudson stirred beside her. He rolled to spoon her, his hard-on as insistent as last night, and he groaned. "Baby..."

"We're still in someone else's home."

"Then come home with me. If you're hungry, I'll buy you breakfast along the way—but I'm only starving for you."

"Okay, should we sneak out?" She asked.

"No. We're thirty, not teenagers, and Summer's parents are cool. Come on, up. Unless I'm pushing and you're not ready for us."

Brook stood and enjoyed the way his gaze slid along her body as smoothly as his hands had through the night. Appreciative, and hot enough to make her more than ready for him. Under the sheets, his erection still jutted, and she almost gave in until she heard murmurs and the sounds of the others moving around. "Do you need a cold shower?"

"I can settle enough to get us home without killing the joy." He threw back the covers for a more impressive view, and when she groaned, he snickered. "Are you sure you can wait another half an hour?"

Still teasing each other, they hurried to dress and popped their heads into the kitchen on their way out. "Thanks for the bed, Mrs Thomas."

"Anytime, honey."

Mr Thomas handed each of them an envelope with too much cash enclosed, and Brook shook her head. "You don't need to pay both of us. We'll split it between us."

"Your songs matched Summer and Ronan—it was perfect, just like the pair of you. You definitely added some life to the party. Are you staying for breakfast?" Mrs Thomas bustled over, wiping her hands before hugging Brook.

"Ah, no. Thank you. Hudson has a place in mind."

"Okay. Have fun."

She followed him back to his home, the man pushing her to break the speed limit. He was unlocking the front door when she parked, and she hurried to catch up. "That was a mad dash."

He turned dark eyes on her, his pupils flared and ready to pounce. "Tell me you're not ready and I wait. Otherwise, the next stop is my bed."

Stepping up to him, Brooklyn began working on his shirt buttons. "I know what I want, so shut up and kiss me."

He interrupted her plans to undress him on the doorstep and lifted her up his body, so she had to cross her ankles behind his back. The bulge straining against his fly perfectly aligned against her and set off a blast of rockets, shortening her breathing to gasps. A slam of the door and he carried her down a dim hallway before he set her down at the foot of his bed and stripped off her dress.

His scorching palm against her belly urged her back to the mattress. "Sit and watch, no touching."

"That's mean." She clutched at the navy doona beneath her, trying to anchor herself.

"The way you ogled me earlier was hot, and you're lucky I didn't lose my load." He finished with the buttons to throw off the shirt and then dropped his pants and boxers to the floor, bending to block her view.

"Ogled? I can't really see anything…"

After dealing with his shoes and pants, he straightened. Now his alignment was even better, and she wondered if licking was the same as touching.

"Brooklyn…" It might've been a warning, but to her ears it was an open invitation, and she circled the crown with her tongue. Hudson sucked in a harsh breath. "You're breaking the rule."

"My hands are on the bed." She held on so tight her nails bit into her skin, but he tangled his hand in her hair to tip her face up.

His jaw twitched as colour rushed to his cheeks. "Put them on your breasts. Show me how to touch you."

Pulling the bra cups down raised her nipples as if they begged for attention, but massaging herself only made her more desperate. Self-consciousness reared up, and she faltered.

"You're beautiful, don't stop." Hudson bent and teased a kiss across her jaw. "All I want is to make you feel good."

"Then you touch me. I'm happy to beg."

So he used tentative strokes like hers, exploring until he grazed a calloused forefinger over her nipple. Her moan sounded like 'more' and he zeroed in on the tight buds with firm tugs. In a flash, he gathered her close and scooted them into the middle of the bed before latching his mouth onto her breast and sucking the flesh deep.

The first promise of an orgasm coiled deep inside, so she patted his shoulder. "Condom, now."

When he knelt above her to reach for the bedside drawer, she stroked the hard length between them and he growled. "Damn it, woman."

The condom tore in half, and he whimpered as he searched the drawer for another. Brooklyn snickered. "I'm safe if you are. No possibility of a shotgun wedding."

Still, he rolled on protection, but before disappointment could curl through her, he searched her face, his smile gentle. "Tempting, but some things are too important to leave to chance. Marriage and family—if we find ourselves on the same page—then we choose to start that life together. Know that we're in it for each other and nothing else. Are we on the same page now?"

"Yes, but you're lagging."

He grinned, then filled her in one hard stroke. The last twelve hours had been enough foreplay, and her core was already slick, almost throbbing in time with her pulse. She writhed beneath him, trying to get closer, and when she raked her nails down his back to grope his ass, he growled.

"Hands above your head." She pouted, but did as he asked, and with her hands pinned under one of his, the other gripped her hip, lifting her to meet his thrusts. Her orgasm rolled through her as they hit fever-pitch before he slowed and throbbed inside her, then released her hands. "Touch me, baby."

"You're close."

"Mmm. Trying not to think about that."

When her fingers snagged his curls, he groaned and his eyes closed. "Again."

He followed up with a thrust so deep she splintered and followed his release with another of her own. After rolling off her, he lingered with teasing strokes over her breasts and along her waist. A shudder rippled through her and he nuzzled into her neck. "Sorry, I couldn't hold back. Next time I'll last longer."

"Don't hold back. So long as there's a next time." Brooklyn burrowed in, enjoying her first real session of lovemaking, rather than the meaningless sex that left her lost or ashamed.

Mumbling, Hudson kissed her forehead. "Plenty more to come."

THE PLENTY MORE BECAME another fortnight, working and playing together so often that she only visited her house to grab more clothes. Hudson had opened more, too, and now he'd finished enough of his music to record an album and he'd played for her a few times. Something still held him back, and she couldn't understand his resistance when he had so much natural talent. Slowly he revealed the highs of his music career, but not why he'd stopped.

Now they were at the beginning of December, and the pub was gearing up for the holiday season. Usually, she avoided the preparations, but this year she wanted some magic for herself. Hudson was into it, and he'd dragged out a singing Santa from the spare bedroom and thrown tinsel over the door handles.

She sat on the bed and watched him dress in his standard surf shorts and a t-shirt while she waited in her work uniform. "Did you want to come to the bar with me and help decorate?"

"Yeah. Do you think you can take Sunday off? My family has a tradition and I..." He raked a hand through his hair, gathering it into a bunch before tying it back. "I want you with me, but you can say no."

"What's the tradition?" Rising, she stepped into his arms, and he relaxed a little.

"Just dinner before we put up the tree. Things will be a little crazier now all my sisters can legally drink." While he didn't come off as a protective big brother like Summer's, his affection ran deep for his parents and siblings. Brooklyn had hoped she'd meet them one day—that she was important enough.

"Not eggnog..." She scrunched her nose.

He shuddered. "God, no. Cocktails—Mum could give Thea a run for her money."

"Will I need to dress up?" She mentally checked her wardrobe for something not black.

Laughter burst from him. "Dinner is fish and chips on the deck, looking over the ocean. Casual runs in my family—Dad wears golf clothes, though. Is that a yes?"

"Yes, please. Is it local?"

"No, Port Stephens. Pack a bag."

"For someone so casual, you're bossy." She teased her hands under his shirt, and he stopped her before she could mess him up.

"You bring out the best in me."

ON SATURDAY, BROOKLYN'S nerves peaked. She'd stopped at the mall this morning and bought clothes she'd never look at twice in the past, as well as a Christmas present for Hudson—another rarity. After hiding it at her apartment, she packed her new clothes in her suitcase and headed into the bar.

When she arrived, she admired their handiwork from a few days earlier: the swathes of blue gum garlands, silver tinsel and aqua baubles clinging to the beams and doorways throughout. Their efforts still stunned her and the swell of excitement hit her again—it would be her first joyful Christmas since her mother kicked her out. That reminder sank her happy bubble.

Ronan pulled her aside. "What are you worrying about? Is the guy giving you trouble?"

"No. I'm meeting his family tomorrow." How accepting would the Wells family be? One with such strong ties, while she'd been set adrift at eighteen.

Ronan arched his pierced eyebrow. "Can't say I envy you. I was lucky I knew the Thomas' before ..."

"Before you knocked up their baby girl and almost wrecked everything." Instant remorse hit her. Not for teasing Ronan, but for forgetting she had found her family, and their ties were just as strong.

"Go easy." Ronan's quick grin flashed. "But yeah, pretty much. Still, I didn't think they'd want me at their table for Sunday roast."

She shifted from teasing and soothed him. "They're not like that."

"No, and I think there are more parents like Summer's out there than ours. Give yourself a chance, Brookie."

"Will you be a Mr Thomas kind of dad?" Brooklyn asked as she straightened a stack of napkins.

"Yeah, for them and Summer, as much as for myself." Ronan darkened for a moment. "You better not be pregnant."

"I'm not. Hypocrite." She wandered off to the office next, just in time to catch Lucas on one knee in front of Tiffany.

Brooklyn should've stepped back and left them to it, but suddenly the other girls flanked her, and Presley tutted. "Seriously? You don't propose in an office."

"I'm practising." Lucas stood flushing, while his fiancée-to-be giggled.

Popping her head over Thea's shoulder, Summer smiled. "Why? Ronan just asked me when I wanted to marry, and I said before the beached whale look. His response was 'soon, then.'"

"Well, you have popped out in the last couple of weeks. Your bump is more ball than largest mammal on earth, though." Now they were all together, Brook filled them in on the Hudson development. "I'm meeting his family tomorrow. For a Christmas tradition."

"Ooh, that's big." Chanel squeezed her in a hug.

Brooklyn knew that, but she wanted their points of view. "Why?"

"Well, you can meet the fam anytime, but specifically for an annual event?" Chanel shrugged. "Big."

"He said they're as casual as he is."

Presley's eyebrows shot up. "Okay... that's a good guideline for how to dress."

"What are you taking with you?" Chanel asked.

"An overnight bag?" That's all Hudson had instructed, but now her worries ramped up.

Chanel pulled out her notepad. "No. Wine, Christmas treats. I have some fruit mince I can whip into tarts for you."

Brooklyn rubbed her temples. "Oh, god. I need to cancel."

"No, you won't." Hudson leant in the door frame, legs and arms crossed.

Thea, the traitor, muttered under her breath. "Nice."

Brook glared at her friends and pushed him back out the door until they were out of earshot. "Sorry. I'm not cancelling, I just panicked. They know more about this stuff than me."

"About my family?"

"No, social skills…"

Hudson shook his head, but a smile emerged. "Do you think I'd throw you to the wolves? I have everything we need to be socially acceptable. They'll love you as much as I do." She stared at his chest, hoping the words were true, even though they weren't an actual declaration. He tipped her chin so their gazes collided. "I love you, Brook, knew my fate the first day we met."

"I love you. My first and last."

"Good, but until you're not afraid that you'll be set aside, I'll take care. I want you too much to mess it up with carelessness."

She threw her arms around his neck and met his mouth. Expected, it seemed, because he needed no encouragement to meet her stroke for stroke and lift her to her toes in a promise of pleasure when they finished for the night.

A squeal interrupted them—Tiffany's—and they all regrouped at her office door. Lucas had her sitting on the edge of the desk, devouring her, and her left hand at the nape of his neck sparkled with square-cut bling. Chanel barely waited for them to breathe before she reefed her little sister away and engulfed her with a hug.

Presley rolled her eyes. "Practice my ass. About time, Fisher."

"I didn't want a freaking audience." Despite Lucas' cranky bite, a smile quickly emerged.

"You were always gonna get one." Ronan strode in, hands on hips. "If you hurt her…"

"Stop it." Tiffany rolled her eyes and hugged their protector.

Hudson chuckled. "This place is the best. Ready to set up for the night, baby?"

"Yeah."

They headed for the stage and argued over the set for a while before she realised what he'd said. "You like my family."

"I do. And I met them ages ago. Time to catch up."

8.
Hudson

AFTER A SLEEP IN AND brunch, Hudson drove them north to Port Stephens. The fifty-minute drive was an easy one that his sisters travelled daily to study. There'd been a time when Hudson thought he'd never want to leave, but as long as he lived close to a beach, he'd be happy.

At a set of lights, he checked over Brook sitting stiffly beside him in cut-off jeans—nice and casual—but the floaty floral top was new and unusual. Hot and alluring, though, with its tiny rosebuds dotting the white cotton. "Do you like that shirt, baby?"

"Yeah, it was an impulse purchase, though. You don't like it?" She tugged at the hem and drew his attention to the cleavage she revealed.

Returning his gaze to the lights, he ran a hand up her smooth thigh. "I only care that you do. Because I never want you to change to fit in with whatever the fuck is socially acceptable."

"I love it, but I also feel conspicuous. Maybe I'll steal a shirt off you later."

That didn't help his fading concentration. "Bloody hell, that's as good as having you naked."

Her laughter bounced around the car and filled him up. She shot him a grin. "Sounds like your standards are much lower than mine."

"I'm merely working on all the times you've stolen my shirt while you're butt-naked."

He still couldn't fathom how the woman who was a vault when they'd first met, had become so open. But he also remembered her words at the wedding: the right person changed everything, and he wanted to be that man. Was certain he could be, even when his history with women was dubious. An apocalypse, plus a stint in rehab, was a few levels up from dubious, though. Hopefully, Mum had forgotten about the fall-out from a few years ago.

Brook squeezed his hand. "Where'd you go?"

"I love you." What else could he say? After the shame he'd fought daily before Brook, he couldn't ruin it now.

"And I love hearing it nearly as much as I love you. Promise your parents won't hate me?" The little waver in her voice calmed him. Uncertainty plagued them both, so together, they'd get through it.

"They're fair, but I've given them a fair reason to doubt my choices."

"Worse choices than a pub singer who works the bar sometimes, and pole danced back in the day."

"No to all of that, and I still want to see the pole dancing." He should've prepared her for the worst of his dating history before now. "I've let women use me, wasn't smart enough to figure out their motive until it was too late. You're different because you try hard not to want anything from me."

"I want everything."

The quiet confession stole his breath, and he squeezed her hand again. "Your kind of everything differs from what my exes aimed for, and I want to give you everything, too."

"I have no interest in your girlfriends' past, but will you let your family change your mind about me? Lucas' parents persuaded him away from Tiff, and it took them a decade to find their way back to each other."

A week without her wasn't an option, so a decade was unthinkable. "There are only two of us in this. Our families are important, but they're the bonus, and our love will be the everyday. More important."

Another half hour, and he pulled into his parent's driveway. Brook inhaled like she was drowning. "Please don't let me mess up."

"Too easy, but don't join the oestrogen gang and take me down, either. Dad and I don't need the scales tipped to five against two." She laughed at the silliness, and he kissed her knuckles. "Just be you. That's who I've fallen for. You match me, share my passion, and care so much you leave me stunned every time."

He wouldn't tell her he was nervous, too. There'd never been a woman important enough to bring home. Sure, a couple had met his parents, but not on home turf, and definitely not during the holidays. His youngest sister burst from the house, trailing tinsel behind her.

Tarni squealed and launched herself at him before she checked over Brook. "Aren't you two pretty together? Mum was catatonic when you sprung the news on her Friday."

"Ignore her, Brook. Tarni's studying drama, so she exaggerates everything." Hudson ruffled his sister's hair and earned a swipe. "Plus, I warned Mum a couple of weeks ago that I might bring you, so you're expected and welcome."

Tarni grinned. "Of course. We've written two pages of questions."

"No." He raised his voice the way Dad did when he tried to be firm. Tried and failed.

Shannon, the closest in age to Hudson, poked her head out. "We culled a heap. And we're curious—you've never brought a girl to the castle."

"Can we come in so I can introduce Brook properly? Pretend we're a normal family for five minutes." He grabbed the box of food Chanel had packed, leaving their clothes for later.

Full of life, Tarni skipped ahead, yelling out to the others. Shannon shook her head. "Welcome to chaos, Brook. I'm Shannon—Hudson's favourite."

"Because there were only us two for six years before the brats came along."

Brook clutched his hand tighter, so he tucked her under his arm. "We'll break the ice, then head down to the beach for a bit."

"I'm okay."

When they reached the kitchen at the back of the house, Cary's attention belonged to piping goop onto little crackers, while Mum dumped olives beside cheese and mystery meats. Dad stopped his pouting and met him with a backslapping hug. "Thank god you're here. They're planning to do something weird with the fish and chips."

"Salmon parcels with baked potatoes—it's basically the same," said Mum as she waved Dad away from Hudson for a tight squeeze. She'd obviously ignored his description of Brook.

"Guys, this is Brooklyn. The girl I told you was minimum fuss like us."

Mum offered Brook a hug, too. "We can mix things up."

Thankfully, Brook smiled. "Chanel has salmon on the lunch menu every Sunday, it's my favourite."

"I have a TAFE assessment this week, the last for the year, and I need to practice." Cary frowned at her work and gave one a poke. "Is Chanel your sister?"

"Questions already..." muttered Hudson.

Brook snickered. "My cousin's best friend, and they're both close to being sisters."

"I wasn't digging for info... what does she do with the salmon?" Cary continued her one-tracked focus. "Everyone will do potatoes of some kind."

"Oh, she serves it with green beans, tomatoes, olives, and anchovies. I try to stay out of the kitchen, but I think she bakes it all together."

Just the mention of hairy fish and Hudson winced along with his dad, but Cary nodded like it made perfect sense. "I'll see if there's something online. So you work at a restaurant..."

"A pub. There's always somewhere I can fill in, but my main role is live music on the weekends." When everyone froze and Shannon groaned, Brook crossed her arms. "I've said the wrong thing."

"It's not the same, Mum. Brook wouldn't be here if it was. I love her—the proper kind, like you and Dad. She's not pushing me with my music, and we both benefit from working together. The girls wanted to switch up the music, and the gigs with Brook has helped me write again." Hudson sighed and focussed on Brook. "Bloody hell, it sounds like I'm using you more."

She'd clammed up a little, but her voice was light. "I don't think you've told me the full story, but if we're willingly giving, then it's not using."

"Leave Brook with us, boys." Mum clapped her hands. "Snacks and drinks in twenty."

"But..." Hudson caught Mum's glare and he gave in, but whispered in Brook's ear. "Run screaming if you have to. I'll get us out of here."

He thought Dad would lead him to the deck, but asked him to his office instead. "Why are you hanging around bars again? If you're writing new music, you should aim to tour again."

"It's not what I want anymore." When Dad shook his head, Hudson held firm. "I'm marrying her as soon as she's ready."

"And pub gigs on a weekend are enough?"

"Brooklyn is everything. Aren't you happy with the work I've done for you?" Hudson's voice wavered. He could never repay his parents' unconditional support and just the thought of letting them down again, sickened him.

Dad sighed. "Of course, but I thought you'd get back out there. You're talented."

"Touring isn't the only way to showcase my talent. I won't waste it again... I know I owe you."

"What?" Dad breathed the word painfully. "Loving you isn't a job, son, and supporting you through tough times doesn't come with a debt. Is this why you stopped writing?"

"The block was mostly shame, but Brook changed everything." He still didn't understand how she'd lifted him out of the darkness, but he wouldn't give her up without a fight.

Leaning back in the chair, Dad linked his fingers behind his head. "How many songs have you written?"

"Enough for an album." A good one, but he didn't need pressure right now.

"Do you play them at the pub?" Dad asked.

"I'm not sure if I'm ready. Brook's heard some riffs."

"Before you think about marriage, you should trust her first." When Hudson slammed down the shutters, Dad backed off. "Send me a demo. Just one."

"Can you give her a chance?"

"I will. Partners don't hold you back, though."

"She won't." Maybe she'd give up on him, though, because he hadn't told her everything.

Mum called time, and they wandered out to the deck. The scorching afternoon had lured families onto Jimmy's Beach, and on the opposite side of the inlet, fishermen patiently waded in the shallows, waiting for a bite. His sisters had sandwiched Brook between them, and he poked Shannon away so he could sit beside her.

"Survived the twenty questions, baby?"

Tarni snickered. "Not even half done."

"We've learnt some disturbing things, though." Shannon elbowed him in the ribs. "You haven't taken her on a date."

"We went to a wedding together." Brook argued without a beat. The twenty minutes must've gone well.

Cary raised a finger. "He hasn't bought you flowers."

"And he doesn't need to." Brook's chuckle warmed him through. She'd not only survived, but blended right in.

"I haven't messed up yet," Hudson argued, then tested a goopy cracker, surprised when it tasted better than expected.

Dad's brow furrowed. "Don't wait until you have to grovel, son."

"Why are you grilling Brook on that stuff?" Hudson asked.

Mum finally joined them and set a platter of mystery meats on the table. "I needed to see if an apology was in order. If my only son had been sent into the world clueless."

Probably a fair call, but he arched an eyebrow at her. "And?"

"Oh, there's no need to worry." Mum waved a vague hand at him. "Brook will pull you up if necessary."

He scored a kiss on the cheek from Brook before she scooped out a spoonful of olives to share between them. "Don't worry, they dragged up dirt on me."

"We're joining her pole dancing classes next year." Cary fussed with the servings, readjusting the food as it disappeared.

"If they go ahead," said Brook.

"Make it happen." Tarni clapped her hands, then reached for their paling father. "Don't have a heart attack, Daddy. It's good exercise, nothing else."

As the teasing banter continued, Brook settled against him, all her earlier tension gone. Once his nosy sisters lost interest in digging for dirt, he relaxed too, except for the worry that he wasn't giving Brook what women usually wanted. His exes had expected lots more, and he'd chased his tail trying to keep up. Brook wouldn't ask, though, and Dad might be on to something. Happy surprises had to mean a lot more than tokens to save his ass.

Eventually the wind picked up, scattering the serviettes and leftover food. They hurried to capture it all when Hudson noticed the storm front hovering darkly on the horizon. "I'm taking Brook down to the beach before we have to hunker down for the night."

"It's moving in faster than predicted," Dad warned.

"Get the tree ready. We won't be long."

They had to walk past a few houses to find the beach access, and on the way, he snapped off a sprig of Christmas bush while Brook texted her cousin. Once they hit the sand and kicked off their thongs, he offered it to her.

Brook blushed, as pretty as the pink flowers. "Where did you get that?"

"I kind of stole it." He tucked it behind her ear before pressing his lips to her forehead. "Looks good on you."

"Stolen goods?" Brook teased, but when he bent to offer her a piggyback, she jumped on and rested her cheek against his. "Your sisters were teasing about the dating stuff. I'm happier than ever, and that's more important."

"It is. Then I realised you don't expect anything from me, and now I want to give you more."

Once they reached the water, he set her down to wade along the shoreline for a while. The gusting winds didn't steal her smile or his joy. They stopped for a while, wrapped up in each other with no words needed.

Brook eventually broke the silence. "Can I ask about your ex? How did she hurt you that bad? Enough for your family's instant horror."

Confession time.

He wouldn't handle Brook ditching him, but it was her call, and he sighed. "We got in deep with drugs and shit, but she handled it better than me. My parents forced me to rehab, and while I was gone, she took my work and ran."

"Did she use it?" While her fingers dug into his biceps, she scanned him with worrying eyes, not horror.

She wasn't running, but the empathy settled him more. "Yeah, with my bandmate. She was the third girl to take advantage of me, but that one hurt the most. Not just losing my work—but getting hooked on drugs to take me that low. I know I'm responsible for my choices..."

"Have you ever lapsed?" Brook murmured, holding him closer.

"No, it never should've happened. My family deserved better." Hudson turned them, and they retraced their path in the shallows, aiming for the beach access.

"You deserved better. And you have to want the change for yourself, no one else."

The easy acceptance dropped his guard, and he knew there'd be no judgement from her. "Yeah, but then you came along. I couldn't write for years because of the shame, and when I managed to get some down, it just sucked. Now I know it's good, but I'm holding back."

"Are you worried I'll run with it?"

"That's the stupid part—it's an irrational fear because I know you won't. That's how sure I am about you."

The surging tide frothed against their calves, but Brook framed his face. "If it takes years for you to share with me, I'll still be happy to hear it. You don't have to get it out there tomorrow."

"Dad wants me to send him a demo. I'm wasting my talent and I should be touring. His words, not mine."

"Oh..." A barrier went up—he saw it so clearly—and she almost pulled away, but stayed close. "Only you can choose where to go with your music. I won't hold you back."

"You set me free."

9.
Brooklyn

WELL, DIDN'T THAT SUCK? Brook bent her head to his chest, willing the tears gone. She couldn't cry over a guy. Had never felt the urge once, but Hudson was different and she was set to lose. The wins in her life were few and far between, but she'd wanted this one to stick.

She should've known better.

"Brook. Come back to me, baby. I'm not leaving you." His voice shook, so she burrowed closer.

"I'm fine." Brook swiped at her cheeks, then met his gaze. "I know how bad relationships work. My father left first—we were holding him back. When Mum didn't support me after the trouble with the manager, I moved in with Presley and my aunt. She's kinder now, but gave Presley hell for most of her childhood. Horrible parenting runs in our family..."

"You're not holding me back, and I'm not wasting time with you. We need honesty, though." The skies opened and fat raindrops pelted her back. Hudson grabbed her hand and turned towards the access point. "Run."

By the time they reached the front porch, they were dripping. Hudson called out for towels, and Cary brought a couple to the door. Hudson braved another run to the car to fetch their bags before they dried as much as they could and wrapped the towels around their bodies. Then they hurried upstairs to a guestroom where he tossed the bags in a corner and dragged her into the bathroom.

His eyes darkened as he bared her, but a glimmer of a pout showed. "I would've liked a few extra hours with that top. No one would notice if my hands disappeared under it." Flicking the tap to hot, he stripped next, then followed her into the shower.

Brook raked her fingers through her hair and almost burst into tears again. "I lost my flowers."

"I'll get you more soon. My neighbour has all those roses." Laughter choked her, and he nuzzled against her neck. "That's better. I love you, and there's nowhere else I want to be."

She tiptoed so his shaft could nestle between her thighs, and he lifted her higher to settle himself inside her instead. When he backed her to the cold tiles, he cradled her head with his free hand and rocked their bodies in a sweet rhythm.

"You don't have protection…"

"Tell me to stop, and I will, but I'm all in. I'll never walk away."

AFTERWARDS, THEY JOINED the family downstairs and found an extra guest had joined them. Once Hudson greeted the guy with a back-slapping hug, he introduced his best friend, Eli, to Brooklyn. Appearance-wise, he was Hudson's opposite and hadn't received the memo on casual.

His dark eyes scrutinised her for too long before they lit with recognition. "You're the girl I didn't set up with Hudson. Not that I'd set him up with a muso. No offense."

"None taken. I understand why you'd protect him."

"Huh!" Eli narrowed his eyes at Hudson. "So, when's the wedding?"

"Dude!"

Thankfully, Cary called them to the dining room for her salmon and roasted vegetables. The men bemoaned their regular fish and chips, while his mum kept the peace. It almost had Brook missing her mother. Hudson and his dad didn't moan for long, and Cary settled when they begged for seconds.

When Hudson was done, he leant back in his seat and rested an arm on the back of Brook's chair. "You should try Darby's fish and chips one night. The girls there are Brook's family, so it'd be good to get everyone together."

"Where are your parents, Brook?"

Oh, no. She'd expected the question, but still wasn't ready. "Last child support cheque from my father was the Bank of Queensland, and Mum's somewhere in Sydney. Spending time with you guys makes me want to find her, but it's been a while."

"Reaching out first takes courage." Mrs Wells rose from the table and gathered the plates as she spoke. "You're young, was it the teenage rebellion?"

"I was eighteen, but she didn't believe me about something serious and I had to protect myself."

"The band manager?" Hudson rubbed her shoulder, and she nodded.

His mum stopped clearing the table and hugged her. "Sometimes mums make mistakes, honey. I'm sure she misses you."

"What's his name?" Eli asked, pressing at his phone. "Between my dad and Hudson's, we could hunt him down."

Nausea rose in her stomach—she wasn't keen on reopening old wounds. "He's out of my life, so there's no need to call in the troops."

"He won't interfere, and he's not calling anyone. Eli's diabetic and keeps track of his carbs every meal. Just a part of his weirdness."

"Thanks, man. So, do you have any hot friends in their thirties?" Eli pierced her with the hawk eyes. "I've never had a chance to bang the bridesmaid."

Hudson groaned. "For god's sake, who invited you?"

The sisters giggled, and Mr Wells arched an eyebrow. Eli simply feigned innocence. "You know I have a standing invitation, and you set the tone, calling me weird."

"Well, my cousin is married, and the only other friend in her thirties would sit you on your ass if you tried that line on her. Thea's almost thirty."

"Nope! No more girls in their twenties. They're only after my body."

Hudson's mum swatted Eli before fussing around at the kitchen bench. "Time to run the slushy machine and fill the margarita jugs."

Once the jugs clattered on the coffee table in front of the Christmas tree, the chatter came from all corners and Brook paid attention to the little traditions. As the tallest, Hudson strung the lights from the top branches while his dad sat in a recliner issuing directions. Eli teased the sisters mercilessly from his perch on a barstool. After Hudson tested the light bulbs, the girls shooed him away to string swathes of tinsel through the needles, and he joined Brooklyn on the lounge.

She settled against him, happy her nerves hadn't stopped her from joining his family and sharing something special. "Do you always get a live tree?"

"Yeah. These days, the farm replants them for the next year until they get too big."

Tarni hopped over and dragged Brook away from Hudson. "Come on, there are some things we don't want the boys involved in. Decorating is one of them."

"Mum always rearranged his attempts." Cary tossed something at Hudson and he caught it with one hand.

The glittery star boomeranged back at her. "They were on the tree. Job done."

His dad fiddled with a CD player on the shelf beside his recliner and Hudson groaned. "Not this time, Dad."

"It's this or the home videos. Have you heard his early music, Brook?"

Before she could ask for the home movies, Hudson grumbled. "She doesn't do pop."

He earned a smack from his mum. "She is the cat's mother. Do you write music, honey?"

"No, I know my limits. I can play most instruments, though."

The questions died off, and Hudson's voice sung from the player. The music didn't appeal to her, and it didn't suit Hudson either, but a riot might erupt if she said otherwise.

Later they lay in bed together with a warm breeze fluttering the curtains. The stormy night had calmed, but empty threats flashed over the ocean. Hudson held her closer than ever, not just physically, and he mumbled against her hair. "You were very diplomatic tonight. Didn't diss my music."

"And I never will. You're talented. I knew it from the first song."

"I've heard that since I was five, so no diplomacy with me. Please."

"I like you in the depths, Hudson. That's where you belong. Is that what you're writing now? More soul?" Brooklyn asked. He'd played some bridges for her, but not enough to get a true sense of the work in progress.

"Dad will hate it."

"Who are you doing it for? I like your parents a lot, but like you said at the Thomas' we're not teenagers. Music and art are expressive—it shouldn't have restrictions."

"Maybe we can have a listening party soon." A heavy sigh followed.

She smoothed the wild curls away from his forehead and pressed a kiss above his frown. "When you're ready. If partners don't hold each other back, they don't pressure them, either."

"I'm glad you came, Brook."

"Me, too."

10.
Brooklyn

THE WEEK BEFORE CHRISTMAS, Hudson hired Darby's back room for an early family dinner so the girls could join in before opening. Later than usual, but once Chanel and Tiffany heard his plans, they'd shifted things around to make it work. Before they left his place, he took her into his studio, leaving his family waiting in the main house.

Brook held her breath as he shifted around to the monitor and his shaky hands clicked the mouse. A guitar strummed an opening riff before Hudson sang through the speakers, deep, untroubled, and perfect. Closing her eyes, she lost herself to him, and let her body slide into the tempo. When he clung to her for the swaying, she opened her eyes on the worrying face, and tried to smooth away the stress lines.

"You're amazing. Do you know how turned on I am right now?"

He flushed and shook his head. "Wasn't what I was aiming for..."

"Well, not from your general audience." She rested her cheek on his chest and listened to the racing heartbeat.

"It's not a duet, baby."

"Because it's your song, and you'll take it wherever you want." Fear flickered through her, but she shut it down. He could go anywhere, but she wouldn't hold him back.

Hudson backed her to the desktop and slid the skirt of her dress up her thighs. "Now you've got me all hot, too. I love you, and there was something I wanted to ask..."

"If I need to concentrate, this might not be the best position." She popped open the bottom button of his shirt to smooth her hand over his abs.

"This position is perfect." Inhaling a rough breath, he covered her wandering hand. "Start the New Year with me, Brook. Move in and if I don't annoy the crap out of you, stay forever."

"What if I annoy you?"

"Impossible. Are you ready for dinner?" When Hudson stepped back to fasten the button, she pouted, and the man chuckled. "I can bet my Gibson that Mum is halfway down the path right now, about to burst in."

"The good Gibson? Oh, I guess there's no point betting on a sure thing." She loved that guitar, but each time he offered her the chance to play it, she refused.

He lifted her off the desk and straightened her skirt. "I'll also bet the thing on us lasting a year without annoying each other. Forever's also a certainty, but you'll be too old to enjoy the win."

Laughter bubbled from her, and she shook her head. "If you can call me old and not annoy me, then I've already won."

"Good try."

They left the studio and Hudson locked up just as his mum reached them. "Oh, we thought you got lost."

Hudson shot Brook a wink, and they headed to the bar. With Shannon in the backseat, they kept the conversation light, no more chatter about moving in and forevers. She was much like Hudson, serenity amongst chaos, and if forever panned out, then Brook could easily see Shannon as a sister like Chanel. Of course, Presley was closer, but she had an edge that few people could pull off. Cary would be the closest to that, while Tarni had Thea's energy.

Forever suddenly seemed possible.

At Darby's, Brooklyn introduced the girls to Hudson's family. His dad seemed more accepting than the first night they'd met—more relaxed and approachable. Thea and Tiffany helped Chanel to deliver the food in time for a relaxed meal together. The Wells women had no problem pumping all the girls for information, and Brook's little family was protective enough to give enough without making his family run for the hills.

After Pat delivered a platter of desserts, Chanel pouted. "This has been the best night we've had since... Hudson turned up. We need to open the doors, but I hope you can stick around. Maybe Brook and Hudson can sing their first hit tonight."

"Ooh, yeah... that nearly melted the paint off the wall," said Thea as she collected empty glasses to return to the bar.

Tarni jumped in to help with the clean-up. "Paint peels..."

"Oh, no, they caused a full-scale meltdown."

Hudson flushed through the praise, but Brook worried. When they were alone backstage, she let him off the hook. "We don't have to sing it."

"No. Match me again and maybe Dad will see me as well as you do."

They hadn't sung *The Dark End of the Street* since their first meeting, and when they broke into it this time it was more cohesive, and hotter. And she fell in love with him even more. If it was possible.

Once again, the Wells' women supported Hudson, but his dad was unreadable. Hudson didn't notice—he was too wrapped up in her. She almost settled, but then Yvette joined the crowd, followed by her mother and the one man she didn't want to see.

She skipped an opening, but caught up, heat climbing from her neck to her cheeks. Hudson didn't let it go. "What's wrong, baby?"

"Mum's here with the band manager."

"No way." He glared out at the crowd, shielding his eyes from the bright lights.

"Protect me. Even if you believe them, protect me... you can forget about us tomorrow."

Hudson turned her to face him, gripping her waist. "Where are they?"

"Yvette's taking them to your parents." She tipped her head to the right. "Kind of looks like Chanel, but plastic."

"Okay, I see them. Let's finish the set."

Unsure if she could trust her voice, she whispered. "Seriously?"

"Are you happy?"

"More than ever." Fear clawed at her, ready to rip away the joy.

"Did you survive when you could've given up?" Tears clogged her throat, so she nodded instead of speaking, and Hudson kissed her forehead. "Everyone knows you're not a backup singer, so stick it to him."

He played a riff to start the next song before more calming words. "Oh, and I'll believe you over anyone, even my parents."

The boost got her through the remaining songs, and they closed the curtains on the dwindling audience. While Brook dragged her feet packing away the equipment, Hudson worked on high-speed. "We'll get through round two and go home. I'm not leaving you."

But only Shannon had stayed for Hudson. The rest of his family had disappeared, and he gripped Brook's hand tight. Shannon stepped away from the tense group and hugged them. "You two are amazing together. Dad had to leave because he really hates your stepdad."

"He doesn't deserve the privilege of that title. That's who I had to protect myself from."

Shannon paled and threw a glance over her shoulder at the intruders. "Oh. Then take us home, Hudson."

"Do you want to talk to your mum? He won't touch you." With Hudson at her back, she braved a nod.

Ronan separated from the group and ambled over. "Who do I need to bounce, Brookie? Other than Yvette."

"If you can keep Mum's husband away from me while I talk to her…"

"Anything for my girls."

Brook met her mother halfway, but kept some distance between them. After twelve years apart the wrinkles and grey hair were expected, and she wore them gracefully, but there was a weariness in her eyes that not even her quiet smile could erase.

When Norm stepped closer, Ronan blocked him, and Mum's face pinched. "I thought when Yvette invited us here that you'd forgotten your silliness."

"Silliness? I'd call it trauma."

"He didn't hurt you."

"He scared me enough to protect myself, so I'll never drop my guard. And if you still think I'm lying, then I'll keep protecting myself from you, too." When tears sprung in Mum's eyes, she relented. "I want you in my life, but if it's another twelve years before we see each other again, I know I can handle it. It's not silly or stubborn—I deserve security with the people I love."

As usual, Yvette stuck her nose in where it didn't belong. "If you two keep working together, we'll need a manager. Darby's will be your home crowd, but I'm sure other clubs will hire you. At least, Hudson, anyway."

Brook laughed, a foreign brittle sound. "Go to hell, Yvette. The only two good contributions you've made in your lifetime are Chanel and Tiffany."

"I'm the owner, and you're lucky you still have a job after those reviews."

"Part-owner." Chanel stepped in to cover Brook. "Whatever Brook was missing, Hudson held the key."

Shannon poked her head around Hudson. "Same goes for Hudson."

"What would we do without sisters, baby? First, how are you an owner? I haven't seen you once in the last few months, so I don't appreciate the interference. And the asshole cowering in the back... come near Brook and I will end you. Dad doesn't usually hate people on sight, so I guess he's heard enough about you to believe fully in Brook. The way I do." Hudson's voice broke a little, and he cleared his throat. "I hope you don't lose another twelve years of your daughter's life because she's something special. Do you have Brook's number?"

"It was in her Christmas card." Mum cast a wary look at her husband, and Brooklyn almost crumbled.

"If you're not safe, Mum, we'll help you start over."

That caused a bluster in the back, and Ronan eagerly saw Norm out of the bar. Yvette shook her head, apologising to her mother. "The girls are burying the business. I'm trying to teach them to use their contacts…"

Hudson scoffed. "Networking isn't the same as using people, and I've known enough users to spot one a mile off. You're one of the worst. We need to go."

"Mum…" Brook wanted to reach out, but the last time she'd tried, her mother had slapped her away.

"Let me talk to Norm." Mum twisted the straps of her handbag between white-knuckled fists. "I'll ring for Christmas."

Heart aching, Brooklyn could only nod. "I'd like that."

11.
Hudson

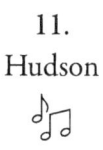

HUDSON WORRIED ALL the way home. There had to be more to Dad's disappearance from the bar than a run in with an old acquaintance. And Hudson had seen the unsmiling response to his and Brook's performance.

Shannon kicked the back of his seat. "Stop brooding."

"Dad doesn't walk away often."

"No, but I promise I've smoothed the way."

Brook tensed beside him. "That I'm not using Hudson, too?"

"Not exactly. Don't want to plant unnecessary seeds of doubt. Just what you told us. He has three daughters, so he'll be on your side."

"It's not about taking sides." Staring out the window, Brook looked ready to break. "People not believing me hurt more."

Shannon leant forward to squeeze her shoulder. "I believe you and Hudson, the most chill man in the world, was ready to take on the world for you. Then you have your posse. How do you get to be one of Ronan's girls? Asking for a friend..."

Hudson shook his head at her in the rearview mirror. "It was his wedding we sang at. His wife is Summer."

"The cute little pregnant one? I wondered if he was a player when they snuck off into a storeroom."

Brook chuckled. "That's regular entertainment in the bar. They think no one notices."

"Mum noticed and she can be a bit airy fairy."

Hudson turned into his drive, happy to see his parents hadn't left. "Dad will probably drag me away for a lecture."

"Take Brook with you. You're obviously in this together, and I know you pretty well. You changed paths before Brook, but she helped light the way. Dad wants us to be happy, so speak up. Take some notes from your kick-ass girlfriend, who spoke up even when no one listened." Shannon opened the car door to slide out, mouth still motoring. "Have a pash and calm down. See you inside."

Brook giggled beside him. "Guess she doesn't know you that well. Pashing doesn't calm us down."

"Nope." Hudson leant across the console and stole a sweet kiss. A quick one that settled him. "You make me fall for you more every damn day."

"It's contagious. I thought our song couldn't get hotter."

"We have a song... nice. I'm thankful I wore a looser shirt to cover the effects. Your pretty dress didn't hide yours, though." He ran a finger over the swell of her breast, wishing they could bypass the chat and head straight to bed.

She gasped, but more laughter followed. "We should head in and get this over with. Do you want an advocate or a silent partner?"

"I never want you silent."

They left the car and hurried inside. His sisters chatted without the worry Mum and Dad wore on their faces. Dad cocked his head to the back. "Can we talk in your studio?"

"No. We'll talk here with our family. I sang with my heart tonight. For my heart."

At his side, Brook stood tall. "And Norm isn't welcome in my life. Neither is Yvette, but we have to put up with her. All I can promise is to protect Hudson, the way he protects me."

"If your writing matches the style you pulled off tonight, then I can only support you." Dad shrugged. "It's a good match, probably not for stadiums, though."

The rushing relief bolstered Hudson. "I want home, and maybe a few niche performances when it fits with our life. We might even have time to visit through the week and mess up your retirement dreams."

"We got jobs tonight." Tarni spoke up. "The chef offered to train Cary for her last year of TAFE and we're both tending the bar during the holidays."

Brook lit up. "That's great, and it'll help get Summer off her feet."

"Chanel was worried about you, too. You work every day," said Tarni.

"They need help..."

"And now they have more. We need a place to stay." Cary arched an eyebrow at Hudson.

He almost whimpered, but Brook answered. "Hudson asked me to move in, so you can use my apartment. Even when you're back at TAFE and uni if you don't have wild parties."

"Daddy?"

"I think the answer's 'thank you', sweetheart."

Mum dabbed at her eyes, always reluctant to let them go, but she hugged Brook. Then she turned on him. "When's the wedding?"

"Gees, Mum. I'm giving her a year to figure out if I annoy her too much."

"Oh, he will," said Shannon.

"I bet the Gibson that I won't."

Shannon rolled her eyes. "Then you may as well pop the question now."

Later, when the family had settled, Hudson had Brook curled around him in his bed, both lethargic. The overhead fan had cooled the sweat from their workout, and this time was more peaceful than the other nights they'd spent together. He stroked her bare back, and she moaned.

"If this is our every night from now on, I'm so in."

"Always said we're good together. Tonight's different." Despite the happiness, his heart still ached for her. "I hope your mum comes around for you, baby. Shannon was right—you're kick-ass. You make me stronger, and there's no shame now."

"You kicked off a few demons for me, too. We still have some hurdles with the bar, but I'm settled now. Secure."

"I recorded a song for you." He'd kept it separate from the rest and finished it with a message. After tonight, he didn't want to wait a year, but he wouldn't rush her.

Brook pressed her lips to his chest. "Sounds like a perfect Christmas present, but it's the same as the others. Whenever you're ready."

"What did you get me?" The question scored him a poke in the ribs.

"That's a sneaky thing to ask when I'm half asleep and prone to telling you anything."

"Surprises are overrated. The only good one I've had is hearing you sing for the first time." He rolled her underneath him and kissed a path down to her stomach.

"Then you surprised me right back. We are good together. I love you."

She tugged his hair, and he groaned. "Looks like I just got my Christmas present."

"And it's never-ending."

12.
Brooklyn
♪♫

ON CHRISTMAS EVE, BROOKLYN left Hudson to his last-minute gift shopping while she helped prep the bar for lunch, and an early close later that night. While the girls shared a coffee, Mum turned up at Darby's with a bruised cheek and hollow eyes. Brook embraced her, rocking them both when she sobbed.

"I'm so sorry, my girl."

"Presley and I had a chat after your visit. We talked to Vivienne..." When Mum protested, Brooklyn held up a hand. "She's your sister. I can rebuild a relationship with you, but I'm also building a life with Hudson, so I still need boundaries."

She settled Mum in Tiffany's office while she called Presley, who answered on the first ring. "Hey, Brook."

"Pres. Mum's here, hurt. Can we call in Viv?"

"Go for it. The office closed early, so I'll be right behind her."

When they hung up, she texted her aunt.

"You and Presley are closer now." Mum sat stiffly in the chair, hands folded in her lap. "Does Vivienne still hold up the bar?"

This could make or break the sister's already shaky bond, so she promoted Aunt Viv. "Mum... she's a regular, yes. Only for lunch on Monday and Wednesday. She offers encouragement, hates Yvette, and makes Ronan blush. An all-rounder."

"I'll try harder. I have too many broken relationships. When Norm insisted I trick you into trusting me, I realised." Mum dug out a tissue from her pants pocket. "You shouldn't forgive me."

"I'm guessing the bruise is because you refused to trick me?" Brook asked. Mum nodded, and Brook hugged her again. "My trust issues are improving, but it'll take a while."

"I understand."

Brook and Presley held their breaths as the sisters reunited over Christmas ham, salad, and eggnog. Vivienne had come in bristling, but the minute she saw Mum's face, tears popped up in her eyes and she smothered her older sister. Now, the brandy in the eggnog had livened them up, and they were joyfully sharing 'remember when' stories.

When Ronan left one of the empty function rooms at the back with a tool belt around his waist, Vivienne almost raised the roof. Ronan glowered at her. "Shirt stays on, Viv. Brook and Pres... much to my discomfort, I've just finished building part one of your Christmas present."

Confused, Brook looked to Pres, who just shook her head. Chanel and Tiffany peeked out of the room and waved them over. "We only installed one, in case you're dead-set against the classes."

At the back of the room, a pole had been set up. Vivienne whooped, but Presley groaned. "I promised Nick…"

"It's classes. Women only. Brook has three keen students already." Tiffany flicked through her notebook and pulled out a mock-up of a flyer.

Since her cousin had shutdown, Brooklyn threw an arm across her shoulders. "You don't have to dance, Pres, but you were the best."

"Of course she was, it's in her blood," said Vivienne.

Poor Presley had shutdown, so Brook shrugged. "If you're not taking it for a test run..."

"I'm wearing a skirt."

Jeans weren't much better, but Brooklyn was up for it. She kicked off her shoes and checked it out, hands on hips, then scrunched her nose at Presley. "He put in crash mats."

Ronan waited just outside the door with his back to the room. "Don't break your neck."

"Why are you hiding, Ronan?" Presley teased now the heat was off her.

"Not watching."

"It's just ballet on a stick, gees." Brook tested the pole, checking the security before she added her weight. A little spin of the bar had her giddy and smiling, so she climbed halfway and tested her strength. She still had it and the balance. It came back like riding a bike, and she worked through a few basic moves, and ended upside down, looking at the women huddled in the doorway.

And Hudson.

Ignoring the cheers, he headed straight for her, eyes narrowed. "That better be my Christmas present, baby, because you'll be hard put topping that. Show me more. No pants."

"We have an audience." She padded across the crash mats to kiss him hello.

He pouted before nuzzling into her neck. "Make them leave."

"Mum's here, too. He hurt her."

He pulled back, serious again. "Well, we promised to help."

"Presley's mum is taking her in while we rebuild the trust."

"You have the sweetest heart." He dropped his mouth to the vee of her shirt, mumbling against her skin. "Have they got the hint yet and disappeared?"

"No, but I'll give you one more preview to tide you over until we can sneak in."

This time, she threw herself into it with a bit more enthusiasm and ended back at the flushing man's feet. "Holy fuck. The classes..."

"Women only."

"Good."

THE NEXT MORNING, SHE dug out the wrapped wooden pick box with the lyrics of *The Dark Side of the Street* engraved around the base. Hudson cleared his throat. "You and me..."

"Always."

"Well, that boosts my confidence." He dug under his side of the mattress and unearthed a ring box. When he flipped the lid, a smoky diamond graced a wide gunmetal band.

"Did I sleep for a year?"

He shook his head and plucked it from the tiny indented pillow. "Read the inscription."

"You and me..."

"We're on the same page, baby. Always."

The End for Now

Keep reading for a sneak peek at Presley's story

Presley

1

Fireworks lit the sky over the Newcastle foreshore and Presley Kelly stood on her penthouse balcony, raising a glass of wine to toast the New Year. Cheers rose from the apartments below, and in the distance crazed dogs barked their displeasure at the booming night sky. Booming and blooming.

In the past, she'd loved the show and the physical jolt to her heart mixed with the joyful hope of a New Year always proved heady. Once upon a time. This was her third alone. She could go to Darby's Bar and hang out with her friends, but she wanted to spend the night with her husband. After all, the fireworks show was one reason Nick had come up with to persuade her to move house.

That, and for hosting his colleagues at the law firm he worked for. They hadn't had one of those either. Not even a party with Darby's girls. They'd moved house and now he worked harder, she was lucky to see him at ten p.m. most days, but she had half an hour to eat breakfast with him.

She shouldn't complain. They had a lot because they'd both worked hard, and besides his kindness and a broodiness that hid a deep passion, his work ethic had been just as appealing. But the ethics had turned into workaholism, and the passion only visited when she pushed him to slow down. The push that preceded an argument before the making up could happen. It was exhausting and not what she wanted in her marriage. All she wanted was Nick.

By one, she was curled up in bed alone when his key rattled in the lock. While her heart lifted, her stomach turned—it happened a lot these days. Like a constant gnawing of fear that if she did get what she wanted it would only be half of what she needed, and it was rare to get what she wanted. The lights flicked off in the lounge and hallway as he headed for their room, and when he stepped into the halo of light from the ensuite he sighed and undressed quickly. Lights out, and he joined her in bed, edging close to press his lips to her neck.

"Sorry I'm late, baby. I didn't get out before the road closures, and then..."

She could fill in the blanks. More work had showed itself and stolen his attention, despite the traffic changes finishing by ten. But she couldn't help turning into his body, craving the closeness and security she'd only found with him. Lazy kisses brushed at her lips, ones that signalled he was asleep on his feet.

"I'm exhausted, Nicky."

"Me, too. If you stay in bed longer tomorrow, I'll cook you breakfast."

She'd rather they both stay in bed and cook breakfast together. Or brunch. But just like the lights flicking off so easily, he fell into a deep sleep, leaving her with tears stinging her eyes, and the lead weight in her gut.

"Happy New Year."

The next morning, she woke to the smell of bacon and eggs. Not her favourite way to start the day, but then the scent of coffee wafted through and coaxed her out of bed. She padded out in her singlet and undies, enjoying the lust that ignited beneath the brooding.

Last year was her entry into the thirties, but she still had the toned body she had when they met eight years ago. When she was a pole dancer, and him one of the crowd. And they would never speak of it again.

He served their too-runny eggs on top of toast and bacon before he kissed her good morning. "I would've brought it to you."

"We can always go back to bed. With no crumbs. Happy New Year."

"Another one." Nick sighed. "What resolutions do you have in mind?"

"To rest more."

"Yeah? That's good, you work so hard. If I finally get a partnership, you can cut back to part time." Oh, god, he was so sweetly clueless. And frustrating. Before she could refine her wish, he rolled on. "I know you need the connection with Darby's, so I wouldn't ask you to quit that. But I keep telling you not to wait on me."

"I'm your wife, it's part of the deal. Who else will take care of you?"

"Me?"

"Do you have a resolution?"

"Just the promotion. I don't know how much more I can work before they take notice."

"What about for home?"

"We have everything I want."

Presley is the fourth novella in the Darby's Girls series, available January, 2025.

Tiffany

1

Tiffany Myers tapped the computer mouse against the pine desktop, but it made no difference. Darby's wi-fi had hit its limit, throttling back to dial-up speeds of a decade ago. Not that the pub had the internet back then—Pop had done everything by the book. Many books. Thick, leather-bound ledgers he'd left for Tiffany and her sister, Chanel, to figure out after his death.

Another smack of the mouse scattered her little tower of beach pebbles, just as Chanel appeared in the doorway with two cups of coffee, steam billowing from the foam. "Did you miss the low-traffic period again?"

"Not hard when the best time to log on is between midnight and six a.m. Maybe I should stay up after the bar closes and work then. At least get the financial stuff through to Presley." Tiffany accepted her favourite blue water-coloured mug and sipped, not caring about the heat. During winter, the old building offered free entry to icy drafts, and no matter how many they blocked, another snuck in.

"She doesn't mind coming in to do the accounting manually. Pres credits her success to Pop's old-school approach." Chanel perched on the edge of the desk. "But maybe we should take the leap and have the system sorted out by a professional. Patrons expect free wi-fi when they visit."

"They expect everything..." Tiffany sighed. Despite the prime location in Newcastle's eat street, their business lagged in most areas. Behind the times like Pop's ledgers.

"Didn't your high school boyfriend study IT? You can hit him up at the reunion tonight."

Tiffany didn't want to think about Lucas Fisher or the probability she'd never get over him. "We were only friends, and I doubt he'd be happy to do anything for me. His sister organised the reunion, and I'm certain she just wants to make a mockery of me, Summer, and Thea."

Chanel set down her chilli peppers cup and grabbed Tiffany's shoulders, bending to meet her eyes. "You're a business owner and awesome manager who works her butt off. Your friends of fifteen years have supported you and they belong here as much as we do, so don't let any of the catty clan bring you down tonight."

"Easy to say when no one picked on you." Tiffany admired Chanel as much as she envied her. Her big sister was the strongest woman she knew.

Chanel shrugged it off. "Of course they did. Now I'm a chef with precision knife skills. And since Pres has been my bestie since high school and owns the sharpest tongue ever, we rule the world together."

"Remember when you brought Presley home from school for the weekend? Mum was horrible to her, but you wouldn't back down." Tiffany would never forget the first time her mother embarrassed them.

"Well, I had Yvette figured out by thirteen and her only concern was image. If we stayed out of the way, she didn't care what Pres and I got up to."

Tiffany nodded. She'd taken a lot more time and heartache before realising the same. Yvette Myers-Northam-Parker had been born thinking she had a silver spoon in her mouth. Nothing could be further from the truth, but she had big dreams of luxury, hence the sister's names. Of all her husbands, Dad had held onto patience the longest, and they were married ten years before she left him destitute.

Chanel kicked her in the shin. "We can't go back, sweetie—only look forward. I've come up with some new dishes for the charity dinner: budget, but fancy."

"Huh. Just like Mum."

Chanel almost choked on her coffee before she broke with hysterics. Settling to wipe away the happy tears, Chanel hugged her, still chuckling. "You're coming along, little sister. Don't feel too guilty later. Oh, and can you add that damn alarm to Ronan's to-do list? I can't handle another three a.m. wake-up call."

Tiffany nodded, and Chanel left her with a smacking kiss on the forehead. She added to the maintenance list, then attempted to refresh the webpage for the hundredth time, her heart heavy. Guilt would hit her, for sure, because where Chanel owned her decisions, Tiffany always had instant remorse for careless comments. Too often she wondered what she'd said to lose Lucas and their six-year friendship.

After battling the internet for another few hours, the bar livened up with the arrival of their friends, and Chanel's coveted barista machine scented the air again. Tiffany wandered out to the front dining area and opened a concertina door to the function room before joining her friends. Thea moaned from her seat, head laid on the table closest to the coffee. "Give it to me, baby. It's going to be a long-assed day and painful night."

"You're so dramatic," said Summer, setting down the bag of mystery garments she'd found for them to wear later. Already in work mode, Summer joined Chanel and finished the coffees while she chatted. "Ten years is a long time, and I'm sure Leah and her lackeys have lost interest in torturing us."

Thea popped her head up to thank Summer for the cream-free espresso shot. "They didn't torture you—tried to steal you from us, though. And no one's lost interest in Leah. Mr and Mrs Fisher almost disowned her after some questionable videos went viral."

"That's horrible. Although she always loved attention." Summer moved on to place a cappuccino in front of a scowling Presley. "Who are you looking to savage?"

Presley added sugar, then stirred the brew into a vortex. "Husband. The usual shit: all work and no life."

"Steve had an overnight trip, but he should be here tonight." Summer's voice lifted hopefully.

None of the girls had warmed to Steve, and with her usual lack of diplomacy, Presley spoke up. "Get out while you can, even if the business trips are legit."

"Pres..." Tiffany nudged her while Summer poured another coffee.

Of course, Presley ignored the warning. "I'm serious. You know I loved how hard Nick worked, but he's becoming obsessive."

Brooklyn rounded out the group of six, and she squeezed her cousin's shoulder. "You work hard, too, Pres."

"Well, helping here is hardly work, and it's not like Nick's waiting at home for me. Where's Ronan?" Presley asked. "That man brightens a woman's day."

Summer almost knocked her coffee over as she sat beside Thea. "You're married, Pres."

"Doesn't matter where you get your appetite, as long as you eat at home," said Presley.

Chanel cackled as she joined them at the table bathed in watery winter sunlight. "Ronan's guarding the door for tonight's event. Are you planning on 'eating at home' tonight, Tiff?"

The sisters had separate self-contained units on the floor above the bar. Independent but not well soundproofed. Tiffany arched an eyebrow at her. "We've discussed the likelihood of Lucas not speaking to me, let alone other stuff."

Recharged by the caffeine, Thea snickered. "There were more guys interested in you besides Lucas. You wouldn't have noticed because you only saw him."

"Yeah, right... let's get this party started. We'll try to keep the lunch crowd away from the back so we can set up," said Tiffany, neatly shifting topics.

But she caught the look between Summer and Thea—doubt mixed with sympathy. Sometimes, her best friends knew her better than Chanel did. Lucas had earned all her attention, and no other guy had come close since. Sure, they'd never officially been a couple, but he'd broken her heart. Later, he'd damaged Tiffany all over again when he refused the invitation to her twenty-first birthday.

After a decade, she wasn't pinning any more hopes on Lucas Fisher.

Tiffany is the first novella in the Darby's Girls series—find it on Amazon: https://www.amazon.com/Tiffany-Book-1-Ella-Sweetland-ebook/dp/B0D46VH5KV

If you loved Summer and Ronan, drop me a line at:

ellasweetland.com
@ellasweetlandromance on Instagram & Facebook
goodreads.com/author/list/19933409.Ella_Sweetland

Acknowledgements

I've met so many wonderful people throughout my writing journey, and I give credit to the wonderful members of Romance Writers Australia for their support both personally and professionally. Their Academy presenters are some of the best, and I give a huge thanks to Sandy Vaile from Fearless Prose. Without Sandy's mentoring and Storytelling program, I'd still be floundering. Special thanks to the members I've met through the various courses, especially Vivian Hanich, Lexi Haven, Ella McLaughlin, and Prue Pearce.

Also, the people who take the time from their own busy schedules to read my work at its roughest – Jo Dennes (my first beta reader), Amber Jakeman, Ella Mclaughlin, and my girl, Keely. Their eagle eyes have spotted typos, dangling plot threads and gaping holes.

Mostly, I wouldn't be here without the support from my husband, kids, and extended family. My husband's support keeps me grounded, and our love can only help me believe fully in Happy Ever After.